Influential as Puck

Lowball Bay Sea Dragons
Book 3

Freya M. Love

Introduction

His entire mission in life is to make me lose my mind.

Blake Eastwood is the team clown. The goalie who never takes anything seriously. The player behind the pranks.

As social media manager for the Lowball Bay Sea Dragon, it's my job to reign him in before he destroys his own career.

After one too many spot fires, we're teamed up to sell the team, while I keep a close eye on him. The guy doesn't want a babysitter, but that's too bad. His passion for lost causes and finding trouble is going to force us together, whether either of us like it or not.

With the playoffs looming, can we work together, or are we pucked from the start?

Tropes:

Brother's team mate, reverse grumpy/ sunshine, golden retriever, hockey.

Chapter One

Alice

"Whose birthday is it?" Andi Welling sat forward, leaning her hands on her desk, her eyes shining as she smiled at me.

"Whose..."

Oh, for real? She was staring at my *hair*.

I ran a hand over it, groaned as more confetti floated off onto the carpeted floor. "Shit... I mean, I thought I got it all."

I'd already spent half an hour in the restroom, frantically brushing it out. Every time I swiped with my hairbrush, there seemed to be more and more of it. The stuff was as bad as glitter.

She smiled, apparently unbothered by my swearing. Or the tiny pieces of paper in my hair that were shaped like dicks. "Let me guess, Blake Eastwood?"

"Who else?" I dropped my hands to my sides with a slap. Closed my mouth just as hastily. Stopping myself before I went on a rant about the team's star goalie.

Andi owned the Lowball Bay Sea Dragons. She was married to my brother, left-winger Cam North. That didn't mean I was free to express my thoughts about the players whenever I felt like it. I worked in the social media department, which made my sister-in-law my boss. I was a lot more dispensable than Blake.

A fact I was acutely aware of, even as I resisted the urge to pick dickfetti out of my brown hair.

Andi sat back and gestured for me to take a seat opposite her. She rested one hand on her heavily pregnant belly. "Do I need to know what happened?"

"Where's Hansel, or is it Gretel?" Rafe asked as he stepped through the door behind me, a steaming cup in each hand. "There's a trail of phallic-shaped confetti all the way from the elevator, leading into here." Andi's personal assistant pushed the door shut with his foot.

I pressed a hand to my forehead and groaned. "Is it that bad?" I swiveled around to take a look, peering between my fingers.

Rafe grinned and placed a cup of tea in front of Andi before taking a sip of his. "Let's put it this way, it's more interesting than a trail of breadcrumbs. Actually, I'm jealous I didn't think of it first. I should leave a trail of cocks behind everywhere I go." He mimed throwing confetti over his shoulder a couple of times.

"No, you shouldn't," Andi told him. "Unless you're going to pay someone to follow you around and clean it up." She narrowed her eyes at him, but the way the sides of her mouth tugged up gave her away. She was trying not to laugh.

He snorted. "Goodness no. Where's the fun in that? So, how did you come to have cocks in your hair?" He sipped and raised an eyebrow at me.

"I found a container of it above my office door when I arrived this morning," I said. It was the perfect way to start a Tuesday. Not.

He grinned. "Ahhh, the old 'container on the top of the door' trick. As soon as you go to move it, it falls. There's nothing like a classic."

"Yeah." I lightly touched my head, grimacing as the tips of my fingers came away covered in more confetti.

"I guess I'm lucky it wasn't paint." And I didn't

get hit in the head with the container itself. Although it was cardboard, clearly not intended to cause actual physical damage. Small mercies, I supposed.

"I think even Blake knows better than to prank someone with paint," Andi said. "Not inside the arena at least." She looked thoughtful for a moment before adding, "Not anywhere there's carpet."

"I was wondering if you forgot the time he tried to paint the mascot on the arena foyer blue." Rafe said, cocked his head, thinking back.

Blake had brought in a container of paint and a brush, knelt down and started to paint over Cee-cee, the red Sea Dragon in the center of the floor. People had walked past, assuming he was supposed to be doing it. That was until some of his teammates arrived, stood around and stared. Drawing attention to his artistic endeavors. He was nothing if not brash.

Smartass.

"How could I forget?" Andi said. "He actually seemed to enjoy cleaning it off afterwards." She shook her head, amused and unfazed by the goalie. Of course, it took a lot to ruffle her feathers.

"He's broken in the head," I said without thinking. "I mean..."

Crap, did I really say that out loud?

Rafe laughed. "He's a goalie. They're all known

for being...different. Personally, I wonder if it's because they take a few too many pucks to the head."

"I hope not." Andi made a face. "I don't want to think they're out there risking permanent damage to their brains."

"Just their bodies and teeth," Rafe teased.

Andi winced. "Sometimes I wish Cam did something else. Something safer. Like skydiving or swimming with sharks." She rolled her eyes playfully.

"I don't think he's done either of those things," I said reflectively.

My brother took risks on the ice every day, but not so much off it. He looked before he leaped into anything. His relationship with Andi for one thing. When they met, he thought she was after him for his money. Which was hilarious when I thought about it now. Andi didn't need his money.

Once he realized that, he opened up to her and they've been disgustingly adorable together ever since.

"He needs to learn to live a little." Rafe sat on the side of the desk. "Even I've gone swimming with sharks."

We both looked at him until he shrugged.

"What? Okay, they weren't sharks, they were sea cucumbers, and they weren't actual sea creatures, they were baseball players." He wiggled his eyebrows at me and smiled.

The Lowball Bay Sea Cucumbers was the city's MLB team, as much a local obsession as the Sea Dragons were. And the Humpbacks, of course, the NFL team.

"I'm sure there's a story there," Andi said. "But I didn't ask Alice here to listen to gossip about other teams."

"Spoilsport," Rafe said, pouting playfully. "Haven't you heard, gossip makes the world go 'round?"

"We all have better things to do than gossip," she said. "Which brings me to why I asked you here today. The Sea Dragons are doing well this season."

This was a safer topic of conversation.

"Yes, they are," I agreed. "The way they're playing, they might just make the playoffs."

Ugh, I couldn't *wait* for my brother's head to swell to twice the usual size. I loved him, but he was insufferable enough at times. Not to mention the rest of the team. I wouldn't be surprised if their combined egos were visible from space.

"That's what I'm hoping," Andi said. "It's the first time in six years if they do. With that in mind, I want to raise the players' profiles on social media.

Something a bit more fun than just sharing a photo here or there. Which is fantastic, don't get me wrong." She raised her hands in front of her, palms out. "You're doing a fantastic job of managing the team's PR. I just thought it would be good to have a bit of fun. Show the world they work hard and play hard."

"Okay," I said slowly. "What do you have in mind?" I had plenty of ideas, but she seemed to be thinking of something specific.

"I'd like the players to pair up and do some challenges for social media," she said. "Have some fun."

She seemed to be hinting at something. It took me a full minute or two to realize what that was.

"You want me to pair up with Blake, don't you?" I resisted the urge to groan out loud.

Yes, she was my boss, and my sister-in-law, but I considered her a friend. I thought she felt the same way about me. Apparently I was wrong.

Rafe pressed a fist to his mouth to suppress a laugh.

Andi looked from me to him and back again. "To be frank, I don't trust anyone else with Blake Eastwood. If he's paired up with another player, they'll lead each other astray."

"What about Flynn Weston?" I asked, knowing I

was fighting a losing battle here. "Flynn can keep him in line. Or Cam. What about Nate Southwell? Or—"

I was officially out of ideas. If they paired Blake with anyone else, they'd end up with more than dick-shaped confetti in their hair.

"I *know* you can do this," she said. "It'll be fun. I'm not asking you to move in with him, just make a few videos and post them online. You don't even need to be in them. Just video him being him and make sure he doesn't go overboard."

His middle name might as well have been 'overboard.' If he could push something too far, he'd do it. If only to see how far he could go.

"I don't have to be in them," I echoed. "I guess I could then." I was strictly a behind the camera kind of girl. Or behind the phone. The others could have all the limelight they wanted. Not me, that was not my thing. Besides, no one would want to see me anyway. I was no one important, just Alice North, social media guru. I was good at what I did, but I didn't need to do it in the public eye.

"Of course you can," Rafe said. Apparently he got over his laughter. "Andi, are you going to pair up with Cam?" He seemed to be issuing a challenge.

"Absolutely not," she replied. "Alice can divide everyone else as she sees fit, but keep me out of it.

I've had my share of Internet fame. Besides, I'll be busier in a few weeks." She glanced down to her belly.

I remembered what she went through when she first took over the team and got together with Cam. I was the one in charge of putting out that particular fire. That was my welcome to the team. Since then, she'd done her best to stay out of the spotlight.

"I have a few ideas," I said. "I think we can have some fun with this. The fans will eat it up."

"That's what I'm hoping," Andi said. "I'd like to attract some new sponsors for the team as well. Keep that in the back of your mind. By the time the play-offs are over, I'd like to have at least three more."

"Piece of cake," Rafe said, apparently more confident in me than I was. "They'll be climbing over themselves to throw money at the team after this. After all, Alice is the best, right Alice?"

"I mean, Grace Hardy is pretty good, but I'm right up there," I said, trying to emulate my brother's bravado. Sort of. I couldn't pull it off, and to be honest, I didn't try hard. Like I said, my place was behind the camera, not in front of it. In the stands, not the center of the ice. The... You get the idea. But a bit of confidence in myself wouldn't hurt either.

"Of course you are," Andi said. "That's why you

work for us. Nothing but the best for the Sea Dragons. I'll let Coach Lampton know what you'll be up to so he can make sure the guys have some time for you. And so they cooperate."

Some of them wouldn't like it, but I'd make sure this was fun for everyone. Including myself, if I was lucky.

Chapter Two

Blake

I loved the buzz of the arena at any time of day. The more people, the better I liked it. Game days were my favorite. The roar of the crowds, the hustle and bustle. Nothing compared to it.

That said, I didn't mind the quiet moments when I'd packed up my stuff, ready to head home either. The calm between the storms, you might say.

I hefted my bag up my shoulder and stepped out of the locker room towards the exit.

"You."

The single word stopped me in my tracks. I smiled and turned around. This should be interesting. It always was. Whether someone had discovered one of my pranks, or took exception to something I said, it was always entertaining.

"Alice North." She was cute, her blue eyes flashing, cheeks pink with annoyance. Standard operating procedure when she was around me.

"Don't play Mr. Innocent with me," she said. She stepped up closer and pressed the tip of her finger to my chest. She looked like she wanted to hit me over the head with one of my sticks.

"Who's playing?" I said with a grin. "I'm as pure as fresh snow."

"You're as pure as fresh something, but it's not snow," she said. She shoved her finger into me harder.

"Newly hatched ducks?" I suggested. "All covered in yellow fluff."

She snorted. "Not even close. Ducks are cute."

I pretended to be offended. "I'm cute." Not as cute as she was, but still. "Did you know you have something in your hair?" I leaned over to take a closer look. "Alice, why do you have penises in your hair?"

She growled, more irritated.

I decided to humor her by staggering back a step or two, as if she was scarier than she was.

"You know very well why I have confetti in my hair." Her cheeks were pinker now.

"Someone got married?" I suggested. "New trend?"

"New trend, my ass," she hissed. "You put that confetti above my door. What did I ever do to you?" Okay, she was more than annoyed now. She actually seemed hurt. Like I targeted her, trying to get under her skin.

I placed a hand over my heart. "I'm shocked you'd think I'd do something like that. Do I really seem like the kind of guy who'd place a box of confetti on top of an open door, hoping it would fall on someone?"

"I didn't say it was a box," she pointed out.

"Lucky guess." I lowered my hand. "I assume whoever did it thought you needed a laugh. Were they wrong?" I cocked my head at her.

"So wrong," she said darkly. "I've been trying to get it out of my hair all day. Andi saw it. How do you think that made me look?"

"Like you enjoy life?" I said. "Nothing says lighthearted fun like confetti, especially when it's shaped like that."

Alice poked me again. "It makes me look unprofessional. What if she thought I didn't take my job seriously, and fired me?"

Okay, that made me stop for a moment. "She didn't, did she?" If she did, I'd be having words with her. Andi was a reasonable woman, she'd understand this was my fault, not Alice's.

"No," Alice admitted. Then she added, "She did something much worse than that. Something both of us are going to regret."

"I don't tend to have regrets," I said. It wasn't like me to dwell on the things I did, unless they ended badly. Which they usually didn't, because my pranks were harmless. No one died yet.

"No shit," she said bitterly. "She wants me to have the players do some social media challenges. Light-hearted stuff to give the fans a laugh."

I perked up immediately. "I love that kind of thing. I'm in, sign me up right now."

"Why am I not surprised you'd be that first to throw your hat in the ring?" she asked dryly.

"Because you've met me," I said. It didn't take people long to figure out that side of me. I was the proverbial open book in that regard.

The expression on her face suggested she wished she hadn't met me.

"Andi wants everyone to do this in pairs," Alice said slowly.

There was more meaning behind her words, but I couldn't quite figure out what it was.

"She doesn't want to pair me with Zack, does she? Because I can't guarantee we'd both survive that experience." The right-winger was as prickly as they came. I'd say he didn't get along with me, but he didn't get along with anyone. He put the grump in grumpy.

"It's much worse than that," Alice said.

"Let me guess." I frowned. I thought for a full minute, but then shook my head. "I can't think of a worse pairing than me and him."

"I can. You and me." She crossed her arms over her chest and glared at me like she wasn't a foot shorter. She reminded me of an angry bunny rabbit. Too cute to be taken seriously unless they bite.

"Do you bite?" I asked.

She blinked at me a couple of times. "Excuse me?"

"Just curious." I've been told I don't need to say whatever's in my head out loud, but it happens. More than I cared to admit, to be honest. Sometimes it got me in trouble, but mostly people thought I was weird. As if being weird was in some way a bad thing.

"So the boss thinks you and I should make videos together?" I mulled over that thought. "I'm still in. It should be fun."

"First of all, it's not like you're being given a choice," she said. "For the record, neither am I. And I won't be in the videos. I'll just be making sure yours are suitable viewing for fans."

"When have I ever uploaded inappropriate social media content?" I asked.

It was her turn to cock her head at me and raise her eyebrows.

I matched her look, but probably wasn't anywhere near as adorable doing it as she was.

"Have you forgotten the dick-shaped balloons you released at the end of last season?" she asked. "Let me start by saying they're terrible for the environment. Not to mention the reputation of the team."

"I'd never release balloons that weren't biodegradable," I argued. "And they were rockets. Is it my fault if you saw something else?" They were totally penis-shaped and I had no regrets about that either.

"Rockets don't have balls," she said.

"That depends on the design," I said. "I stand by what I said."

"What about putting lemon juice in the opposition's water bottles?" she said. "Some people are deathly allergic to citrus. What if one of them was and they had a reaction?"

"I checked," I said. "None of them were. Only an irresponsible person would take a risk like that."

"Funny, that's exactly the word I'd used to describe you," she said. "If you weren't so good at stopping pucks, the team would kick your ass out."

"You think I'm good at stopping pucks?" I asked slyly.

She rolled her eyes. "You don't need me to stroke your ego."

"Not my ego, no," I said, vaguely scratching my ear. Of course, now I was thinking about her stroking another part of me.

"Never going to happen," she said. "We're going to make social media videos that will entertain people without you looking like a total clown. That's it. Nothing more, nothing less."

"What if I want to look like a total clown?" I asked. "You have to admit it's on brand for me."

She closed her eyes and shook her head. "Fine. Let me rephrase. We're going to make videos, and I'm going to make sure you don't injure yourself or someone else. Or the reputation of the team."

"Huh, is that what this is about? You're afraid I'm going to do something that'll make the Sea Dragons look bad." I wasn't sure what I thought about that. I admit to getting carried away once in a while, but no one seemed to mind much.

"The thought crossed my mind," she said, giving

me the side eye. "Andi thinks you need to be babysat. And she's delegated me to do that."

"I don't need a babysitter," I said.

"Finally, we agree on something." She made a face. "But neither of us has a choice here. We have to work together until the end of the playoffs. Andi wants more sponsors and we can't do anything that'd risk putting anyone off."

I confess to wanting to win the Stanley Cup as much as the next player, but the idea of working with her until we were eliminated made me want to win even more. Maybe she was right, I was out of my mind. Why would I want to work with a woman who clearly hated my guts? Apparently I was a glutton for punishment, but she *was* adorable.

"Does Cam know about this?" I asked carefully.

Her brother wasn't just a teammate, he was my friend. And he was protective of his sister. He knew what we were like. Good teammates and friends, but as far as boyfriend material went, we tended to be lacking. Some of us more than others. Take Nate Southwell for example. He used to be up to his eyeballs in puck bunnies. If he looked at Alice the wrong way, Cam would have had something to say about it. Of course, now Nate was loved up with Oaklyn, proving even a guy like him can change his ways. I won't lie, I didn't believe it at first, but he proved me wrong. Good for him.

"Why does he need to know anything?" she asked. "We're working together, nothing more."

"We'll be spending a lot more time together," I pointed out.

She gave me a 'don't remind me' look before tucking some hair behind her ear. "It's just work. I don't need to give him my permission to train with you."

"Would you?" I asked. "Give him your permission, that is."

She was right, he didn't need it, but like always, I was curious. Honestly, I wasn't used to people disliking me the way she did. People always liked the class clown, or at least had a good laugh at them. Looking at me like she didn't want to be around me was new and unsettling.

"The confetti wasn't meant for you," I said. "One of the cleaning staff and I have a running prank thing going on. They were supposed to find it. I guess they did and they left it there." That's the kind of thing Jesse would do. He'd have a good chuckle knowing someone else would be caught.

Alice didn't believe a word I said. That much

was obvious by the way she glared at me while raking more of it out of her hair with her fingers.

"Here, let me help." I raised a hand to brush away a few pieces she missed.

Her hair was as soft as I expected it to be but I didn't expect the jolt of lightning that shot through me.

It must be the static that made the paper cling to her hair. Yeah, that was it. It wasn't physical attraction towards someone who couldn't stand me. No way.

"I've got it," she said. She stepped away from me and shook her head, dislodging more of the confetti. "I need to go home and wash the rest of it out."

Now I was picturing her naked under the steaming water. Okay, there's a *slight* possibility that lightning bolt wasn't static.

You need to stop that right now, I told myself. *Not only does she hate you, Cam would hate you if you hurt his sister.* He was the last person I wanted to get on the wrong side of. Cam North could hold a grudge like no one I ever met.

It was just until the end of playoffs, then we could go back to only seeing each other now and again. I could survive that long.

Right?

Chapter Three

Alice

"HAVE YOU NOTICED HOW INFURIATING MEN are?" I tossed my bag on the hall table and shut the door behind me a little harder than intended. I winced at the bang, but resisted the urge to open it again so I could close it softer.

What was the point, really?

"I might have noticed once in a while," Vivian agreed. My roommate was everything I wasn't. Tall, blonde and a gourmet chef. Even on her days off, she could be found in our kitchen testing out recipes. Lucky me, I got to be her guinea pig.

"I'm sorry." I pulled a stool out from under the island and sat. "I didn't mean to be a downer."

She looked over at me from where she stood stirring something in a big pot, and smiled. "If you're a downer, I'd tell you about it. You're not usually this worked up. Who do I have to put in my pot this time?"

She was right, I wasn't usually so worked up. I shouldn't let him get to me, I *shouldn't*, but Blake always made my blood pressure spike. No matter how irritated I was, he never took it seriously. I'd bet he was looking forward to making those videos with me.

"Blake Eastwood," I said as if that explained everything.

"The hot goalie?" She glanced back into the pot and went on stirring.

"If you'd call him hot," I said with a shrug. I supposed he was attractive in a 'drive me up the wall' kind of way. If a person could look past his ego and ridiculous pranks.

"I'd definitely call him hot, but I guess you don't." She scooped a spoonful of sauce and took a sip from the edge. "Not bad if I say so myself." She threw in a handful more herbs and kept on stirring.

"He's infuriating," I said. I told her about the confetti and the social media videos, fully expecting her to laugh her head off. Vivian was sweet and enjoyed life as much as Blake did, but her enjoyment involved much less humiliation of other people.

"Dickfetti," she said with a laugh. "You have to admit that's funny. I mean, it's a shame you got caught in a prank meant for someone else, but still."

"You know what they say, practical jokes are the lowest form of humor." I exhaled slowly. "I like a good joke as much as the next person, but not at the expense of someone else. At some point, enough has to be enough, y'know?"

She tried a bit more of the sauce and nodded to herself before setting the spoon aside. "Good thing he has you to keep him in line. That's the idea, right? Or is it the other way around?"

"I do not need Blake Eastwood to keep me in line," I argued. "The problem is, I don't know if I can keep him under control. He's...a lot."

"Would you prefer your boss pair him up with someone else?" she asked. "I'm sure there's lots of women who wouldn't mind babysitting someone like him."

"He doesn't need a puck bunny encouraging him." I didn't want to think about the NSFW content they might produce together.

"If I didn't know better, I'd think you don't want to share this guy." She opened the cabinet, pulled out a lid and placed it on top of the steaming pot.

I grimaced. "I am not interested in Blake Eastwood. There's no way in the world I'd go out with another hockey player. Not after the last time."

She knew what happened before; she was there to help pick up the pieces. She and I went to high school together and stayed in contact while I went to college and she studied cooking. After we graduated, we both needed a place to stay and someone to share it with, so we moved in together. It worked out well, for the most part.

"What if he wasn't a hockey player?" She pulled out two wine glasses and poured white wine into both before handing one to me.

"I still wouldn't be interested," I said. "I couldn't live with someone knowing I might get up in the morning to find plastic wrap over the toilet bowl, or glitter in the salt shaker." Exactly the kind of pranks he'd pull.

"He wouldn't do those things to you, would he?" she said.

"He said the confetti was meant for one of the cleaning staff, but doesn't mean it was," I said. "I think he did it to me because he thinks I need to lighten up."

"Do you?" she asked.

"If that confetti fell on my brother's head, I'd laugh my ass off," I said. "Same with the plastic wrap and the glitter. As long as it doesn't get out of hand, I don't care what they do to each other."

"Just to you?" she asked.

I groaned and covered my eyes with my hand. "Maybe I do need to lighten up. It's only confetti, right? It's not like a tub of mayonnaise fell on my head. Or worse, ketchup."

Now that would have been messy.

Vivian shrugged. "You feel how you feel. Some people hate practical jokes. Some people watch shows about other people being pranked."

"They do, don't they?" I lowered my hand and looked back at her. "You don't think Andi meant for me to video those pranks, do you?"

"I think she knows you're the best at what you do and you'll make the right call one way or another," Vivian said. "If you did, you could make sure things went down right."

I shook my head. I didn't know how to feel about any of this. Was it too late to tell Andi I couldn't do it?

Of course it was, and this was my job I was talking about. She had faith in me that I could do this. That's what I'd do. I'd prove her faith in me wasn't misplaced.

I reminded myself all of this was only until the

Sea Dragons were out of the playoffs. I wanted them to win almost as much as they did, but I was already looking forward to it being over.

"Knowing you," Vivian went on, "you've already started making a list of challenges for everyone to do."

"Am I that predictable?" I asked.

"Well..." She filled another pot with water and turned on the heat underneath it. "It's only because I know you so well. You like to be organized. So, what's the first item on the list?"

"Would it be too old-fashioned to start with the ice bucket challenge?" I tried to hold back a smile.

"You just want to see Blake dump a bucket of ice cold water on his head in the middle of winter," she said with a laugh.

"Maybe I do," I said. "But you and I both know he'd do it. He'd laugh the entire time."

"You could make it something other than ice," she suggested. "Or make him think it's ice, but it ends up being warm water."

I was totally not going to imagine Blake immersed in comfortable warm water, especially without a shirt on. No way. I was definitely not going to picture it trickling down his firm chest and hard abs.

Ugh, yes I was. What was wrong with me? He drove me up the wall, I shouldn't be thinking about him at all, much less like *that*.

"That gives me an idea," I said. I pulled out my phone and made some notes.

"Why do I think he should be more worried about you than you are about him?" Vivian asked.

"I'd never do anything that would put him or the team's reputation at risk," I said easily. "But that doesn't mean we can't have some fun."

"Of course it doesn't." She pulled homemade pasta off the rack, where it was drying, and dropped it carefully into the pot of boiling water. "I've seen things people get up to online. The possibilities are endless."

"Exactly," I said. "And they don't have to be ridiculous either. By the time I'm done with him, people are going to think Blake Eastwood is an angel."

"That'll teach him," she said with a grin. "He'll never dare to prank anyone again once everyone thinks he's nice."

"Ha ha," I said sarcastically. "I'll just prove to him he doesn't have to prank people to be noticed."

"Is that why you think he does it?" she asked. "For attention? I would have thought a professional hockey player gets plenty of that already." She pulled out a couple of bowls and forks, ready for dinner, and placed them beside the stove.

"Who knows why anyone does anything." I said. "If nothing else, maybe I'll keep him so busy he won't have time to pull anything new."

"Are you sure you're not the one who wants to pull something?" she teased. "And by something, I mean his—"

"I know what you mean," I said quickly. "I definitely don't want to pull any part of him, including his leg. This is work, that's all. In a few weeks, we'll be done and in the off-season. We'll hardly see each other." He'd be off to visit family and rest, and I'd be working.

I was totally *not* disappointed at the idea. That twinge inside my chest was something else. Probably hunger because the food Vivian was making smelled so good.

Yeah, that was it. It was my stomach, not my chest.

That was my story and I was sticking to it.

"If you say so." Vivian slid me a skeptical look. She drained the water and placed pasta and sauce into the bowls. "You should like this. It has extra truffle paste and mushrooms."

"You know me and my relationship with umami." I sniffed the steam wafting off the food as she placed a bowl in front of me. Chunks of beef and potato were nestled between the mushrooms, sitting on top of the fresh pasta.

"Could anyone learn how to make pasta?" I asked. "You make it look so easy, but I'm guessing it took practice."

"Did that just jump to the top of the list?" she asked. "I can give you some pointers if you want."

"I'd love some," I said. I'd like to learn for myself, but also for the greater good of the Sea Dragons' social media accounts. Fans would eat it up, so to speak. And if I got a meal for my trouble, then where was the harm?

"I think Andi Welling might have created a monster." Vivian sat down beside me and dug her fork into a chunk of beef. She smirked at me before putting it into her mouth and chewing.

I followed her example, my eyes widening how delicious her food was. She'd never made anything that wasn't incredible. When she chose to become a chef, she definitely found her calling.

"So good. And I promise to use my new powers for good and not evil. Just be sure you're following the team. In a few days, I'm going to be uploading a bunch of fun posts."

"I'm already following everything," she said. "I can't wait to see what you come up with. You know if you need any help, you only have to ask. I feel like I'm invested in this now too."

"I'll definitely keep you in mind," I said. "Now I have to figure out which of the players I'm going to pair up." That was going to be a challenge in itself. Not all of the guys got along, and now was not the time to cause conflict or upheaval.

Which actually gave me an idea for my first video.

Chapter Four

Blake

"You want me to choose who's paired up with who?"

Alice appeared in front of me just as I stepped off the ice after a training session. Her usual 'let's get this over with as quickly as we can' expression on her face. The one specifically reserved for me.

"No, I don't want you to choose," she said slowly. "I want to film you pulling the names out of a hat. Not literally a hat." She held up a plastic container full of folded pieces of paper and shook it.

The rest of the guys watched us as they filed off the ice. I decided it was a good thing Cam wasn't here right now. That would account for her timing. She didn't want her brother hanging around, making assumptions.

"Now?" I pulled off my helmet and tucked it under my arm before taking my gloves off.

"Why not now?" she shrugged. "You look good like that." She caught herself and color rose up her cheeks. "I mean, with all the goalie padding on, you look the part."

"You mean because I'm dressed like a hockey player, I look like a hockey player?" I teased.

"Something like that," she said with a long exhale. "Fans will love it."

"Do you need me to put my helmet back on?" I asked.

"I think it's better if they can see your face." She quickly added, "So they know it's you."

"You were about to say so they could see my good looks, weren't you?" I cocked my head at her and smiled.

"Not a chance." She pushed the container toward me and pulled out her phone. "Even if that was true, saying it would be unprofessional."

"Ouch," I said as if she stabbed me right through the heart. I took the container and peered inside. "Are you sure about this?"

"Why wouldn't I be?" She tapped on her phone screen to ready the camera.

"I don't know, but it might be more fun if I pulled these out of my helmet," I said.

She stared at me for a moment. "Right. That's a... That would work."

"I don't mind if you want to tell me it's a good idea," I said with a smile. "My ego is small and fragile." Okay, I deserved the snort she gave in response, but it wouldn't hurt to give credit where it was due, right?

I handed her my gloves and tipped the pieces of paper into my upturned helmet before giving it a good shake.

"Can I ask you a question?" I asked.

"Can I stop you?" She placed my gloves and the empty container aside and stood with her phone in her hand.

"Usually not," I admitted. "Do you want me to do this so the guys blame me for who they're paired up with?"

She cleared her throat and held her phone up in front of her face.

"That's not a no," I pointed out.

She lowered the phone and sighed. "I thought this would be fun, that's all. If you don't think so, I'll come up with something else." She started to turn off the device and step away.

"No." I put out a hand to stop her, my fingers connecting with the fabric of her red sweater. I swear I could feel the warmth of her skin right below the wool, the connection between us hot enough to singe the yarn.

"It'll be fun. And none of the guys can complain about who they get stuck with. It'll be pure luck. They'll have no excuse for giving you a hard time." And I didn't want her to walk away from me, especially not when she was angry. Or irritated. Or annoyed. Or any number of negative emotions I seemed to evoke in her whenever we were together.

Okay, I admit it. I didn't want her to walk away at all.

"You think that'll stop them?" she asked, slowly stepping back. She touched her sleeve as if she also felt the heat there.

"We have witnesses that this is fair and equitable," I said. "Nate, get your ass over here." I jerked my head to the side until the defenseman stepped off the ice towards us.

"What am I being dragged into?" Nate asked, not looking too worried. Of course he wasn't. He followed me into trouble from time to time, but always as a sidekick, never the main perpetrator. He knew better than to get in too deep with anything over the top. That was my wheelhouse. He had limits. I'd yet to find mine. Assuming I had any at all.

'No limits and no filter,' my mother used to say. Okay, she still says that, but now she says it in a way that suggests she's accepted it.

"Just stand there and watch," I told him.

He clapped a hand over his eyes. "Whatever you're about to do, I don't think watching is appropriate." He grinned under his fingers.

"Don't be a doofus," I told him. "I'm pulling pieces of paper out of my helmet."

He spread his fingers and peered between them. "That's it?"

"That's totally it." Alice looked at the end of her patience. "It's no big deal."

"Right, no big deal," I said. If I really had an ego, it might sting a little right now. I couldn't explain why. It *shouldn't* be a big deal, but I liked that she sought me out for this.

Sure, Andi wanted us to work together, but Alice could have done this herself, or delegated it to someone else. But she brought the idea to me.

Don't read anything into it, I told myself. It's not about you. Unless she really wants the guys pissed off at you for picking their name out at the wrong time.

Alice didn't like me, but I honestly didn't think

she was vindictive like that. Not when it might cause trouble within the team. It was literally her job to prevent exactly that.

"Okay let's do this." Back straight, I looked directly into the phone's camera, ready for her nod to go ahead before pulling out the first piece of paper. I unfolded it carefully and read the name.

"Nate Southwell. You're going to be paired up with..." I pulled out another piece of paper and opened it. "Cam North."

"Hell yeah." Nate pumped the air with his fist.

I glanced at him and grinned before pulling out the next pair. "Zack Reed and Sveinn Albertsson." That worked out well, the Icelandic player was one of the few people who could tolerate Zack. They might get through it without killing each other.

"Next up we have Flynn Weston and Valentina Ortiz." I slid a glance to Nate, who had wide eyes and was trying to hold back a smile.

Flynn was the team's center and captain, and one of the most put together guys I ever met. For some reason he wouldn't explain, he didn't seem to like the assistant coach. Personally, I admired Valentina. She knew her stuff. That was all I needed in a coach. We had a shot at the Cup because of her. Because of Coach Lampton too, but her coaching style gave us the edge we needed. Or the kick in the balls.

"Next up..." I went on pulling out names until my helmet was empty and Alice lowered her phone.

"This is going to be interesting," Nate said. "I can't wait to see what our first challenge is." Like me, he was always up for a bit of fun. Although these days they involved his girlfriend and their foster kids, he hadn't forgotten how to have a good time.

"You'll find out soon enough," Alice said. She was squinting at the screen, watching the video.

"Is this where you tell me we have to do it again?" I asked, half-joking.

If she did, I would have. Over and over until she was satisfied. I wanted her satisfied. Lying in a bone-less puddle in my bed—

Where had that thought come from? Wherever it was, I needed to tuck it back in. I could revisit it when I was alone, not in front of her. Alice gave me the impression she could somehow read my mind.

Okay, she probably couldn't, but being an open-book type of guy, she'd see it on my face. She probably saw it right now. Judging by the look she gave me, she knew exactly what I was thinking.

"No," she said quickly. "I'll edit this a bit and it'll be fine. You'll all get the address for the first challenge after I've uploaded it. I expect you all to be there. Okay?"

She gave me a look as if she was sure I'd skip out for some reason. Even stern she was beautiful. Her eyes were so blue, I wanted to dive in and go for a swim. I might never come back out again. And her plush lips, set in line the way they were, they still looked soft and kissable.

Stop it, I told myself. *She asked you a question.*

"I'll be there," I said with as much enthusiasm as I could muster without looking like a golden retriever begging for a treat. I'd told her I was in, but she didn't seem to believe me. Or she thought I'd look for the first excuse to run.

On the outside, I didn't take a lot of things seriously. On the inside, when I committed to something, I was a hundred percent there. She must have seen that about me, at least on the ice, right? She knew I wasn't all about clowning around and pulling pranks.

And yet, that seemed to be what she saw. To be fair, it was what most people saw. Exactly what I wanted them to see. Blake Eastwood, jokester. Guy who enjoyed life.

Judging by the expression on Nate's face, golden retriever and team jester was exactly what I looked like. He had a knowing smile on his lips, as if he was some kind of matchmaker who had a hand in paring us up.

I was almost certain this had nothing to do with him. Although, I made fun of him when he said he was smitten with Oaklyn and was going to give up the puck bunnies. I hadn't meant to, but I pissed him off for a while. If this was his idea of revenge, he'd waited a long time for it. Honestly, I didn't think he had the attention span. I know I didn't.

"I'll go and get changed." He jerked his thumb toward the locker rooms. Of course now we were done, he wanted to make an escape. Oaklyn was probably waiting for him downstairs. Since she was almost as cute as I was, it made sense that he'd be in a hurry.

"Yeah, me too," I said. "If I'm excused?" I grabbed up my gloves and arched an eyebrow toward Alice. I was hoping she'd find it funny, or endearing, but she didn't even seem to notice. Tough crowd.

Her eyes were still on her screen. "Yeah, you can go." After a moment she added, "Thanks." She glanced at me and nodded.

"Any time," I said, lighter than I felt. I could have been back at school being dismissed by a teacher. But this teacher was gorgeous, smart and couldn't stand me.

The universe had a sense of humor. Or Andi did. What was she thinking, pairing us up? Should I go to her and ask her to reconsider? Alice might have more fun with Nate or her brother than with me. Or maybe Flynn. He was nice. Solid. Reliable. Single.

The idea of them working together made a totally unexpected spike of jealousy shoot right through me. Flynn was my friend, but I didn't want him to get close to Alice. The thought of them together, it made me want to put mackerel in his ice skates.

I may do that anyway.

No, Alice was my partner for this. We'd see this through to the end. She might even like me once she got to know me.

Chapter Five

Alice

FORTUNATELY, DOUGHBALLS BAKERY WAS ACROSS the road from the arena. An easy walk for everyone, no excuses for anyone to try to duck out.

Unfortunately, that meant a contingent of curious staff followed us over for a laugh.

The bakery closed to the public for a couple of hours during a quiet time of day. Right then, it was packed full of muscular hockey players who were used to taking up all the space they could.

"This is all my sister's idea, don't blame me," Cam said louder than necessary. "I would have gone to the pet rescue to pet some puppies."

"Nate would have gone for the pussies," Blake said. "I meant kittens," he said before Nate could round on him.

I was well aware of the change in Nate, but apparently Blake couldn't leave that chestnut well enough alone. I glared at him, but he just grinned back at me with his stupid, adorable smile. Why couldn't he look like a potato? That would make this so much easier.

"We know what you meant." Cam offered Blake a fist bump.

"Don't encourage him," I said.

Cam turned to me and raised an eyebrow. "Why not?"

Crap, now everyone was looking at me. I turned away and hurried over to Ian, the owner of the bakery.

"Thanks for letting us do this. The Sea Dragons appreciate your time and support." Of course, this was the kind of publicity for the bakery money couldn't buy. Hopefully it would make up for the mess the guys were about to make.

"Anything for my favorite team," Ian said. "Besides, this is a skill everyone should have."

"We're already good at eating cake," Cam said. Apparently, he wanted to take this opportunity to show me up as much as he could. Possibly to cover his nerves at being involved with social media. He had a love-hate relationship with it, like many people. He hated it and it loved him. Since this was his wife's idea, he couldn't avoid it.

The rest of the guys laughed, except Zack Reed, who looked as though this was the stupidest thing he ever heard. Beside him, Flynn Weston looked just as impressed, keeping as much distance between himself and Valentina as he could. Which wasn't much, given the small space.

"You're not here to eat cake," I said. I nodded to Ian to tell them what they were doing.

"Alice asked me to teach you how to make bread," he explained. "We'll do this in two groups, with one group filming their partner before we swap over."

"Making bread?" Cam frowned at me. "Have you forgotten my relationship with flour?" He had the same relationship with it that I did with confetti, which I was still washing out of places it shouldn't have been.

"I think it's a great idea," Blake said loudly. "You might even learn something, Cam."

My face heated at the way he stood up for me, but Cam stared at him, frowning.

"What did you do, Eastwood?" Cam demanded. "Did you put her up to this?" He waved a hand roughly in my direction before turning to me. "He put you up to this?"

"A minute ago, you said it was all her idea," Nate pointed out.

Cam turned his frown to him. "That was before I found out what we were doing."

"Can we focus on what we're here for?" Flynn asked, at the same time as Valentina said, "Can you be quiet and listen?"

Now he glared at her, while she seemed to be ignoring him.

Great. If this went any worse, I might be looking for a new job. It was supposed to be fun, not divisive.

Before I could say anything, Ian stepped forward. "I have stations set up for all of you with bowls and ingredients. If you'll choose one, we can get started."

I shot him a grateful look. I should have realized bringing a group of hockey players over here would be like herding cats. I didn't know how Coach Lampton did it. Or Valentina, for that matter.

Fortunately, everyone shuffled over to a spot with minimal fuss and elbowing each other out of the way. Blake took the spot next to Cam, with Nate and I on the opposite side of the table so we could film.

Cam shot me a glance. "If you planned to have anyone throw flour at me—"

"I haven't," I said.

"Maybe you should," Nate said.

"I volunteer as tribute." Blake picked up the cup of flour from the table and flicked it at my brother.

Cam ducked, leaving the flour to land on Valentina, who stood on the other side of him.

"Oops." Blake put down the cup and hurried to brush flour off her sleeve.

She put up a hand to stop him. "I can manage, thank you." She gave him a stern look that made him back up quickly.

Cam rose to his feet, putting a hand on the table to steady himself. "Shit, I'm sorry." He turned his head to glare at Blake and me.

I raised my hands to either side. "That wasn't my doing." Leave it to Blake to find a way to get me in trouble. Was he *trying* to get me fired? Maybe he hated this idea as much as my brother did and this was his way of trying to get out of it.

"It was all me," Blake said. "Lay off her, bro. Let her do her job."

Cam looked at him suspiciously again, but stepped back into his place as Ian started showing them how to mix the flour, yeast and water and knead the dough.

Thankful for a few moments of peace, I stepped back into the corner, my phone on Blake as he tried to follow Ian's instructions. Mostly, he ended up spreading flour everywhere. He seemed to have a knack for making a mess without trying. Somehow, he had a bunch of it on one of his ears and more on the tip of his nose.

I was absolutely not noticing how adorable he looked. No way. He definitely wasn't getting to my lady bits either. Not looking messy and certainly not after standing up for me twice.

Okay, I hadn't expected it and I'd liked it more than I should have, but I shoved it out of my mind and focused on filming him and keeping an eye on the others who seemed to be making slightly less of a mess.

Valentina was making bread like she'd done it her whole life.

Surprisingly, so was Zack. His spot was almost immaculately clean and his dough looked perfect. If I didn't know better, I'd think he was enjoying himself. He seemed lost in his own world, focusing on kneading and shaping the dough. I didn't know him very well; for all I knew, this was what he did for relaxation. Why not? Kneading dough was a good way to let off steam, and fresh bread was delicious. There were worse ways to unwind.

"I hope you're not going to eat that," Blake said, nodding towards Cam's attempt.

"Mine looks more edible than yours," Cam retorted.

"Mine is *very* edible." Blake turned to me and winked.

My face heated. He was not referring to the bread he was making. Damn it, I'd need to cut that out of the final video. It wasn't suitable viewing for all ages by any means. On top of that, now I was thinking about his dick, wondering how he'd taste. Imagining him moaning...

Stop it, I told myself. *It's never going to happen. It can't, for so many reasons. He's a troublemaker, remember?* His cum was probably full of glitter. Was that even possible? I didn't know, but if it was he'd find a way.

"Bro, are you flirting with my sister?" Cam narrowed his eyes at Blake.

"Would I do that?" Blake asked, all innocence.

"Not unless you want itching powder in your helmet," Cam told him. He actually gave me a sideways look too, as if I'd done or said anything to warrant being flirted with.

He should know by now I had no intention of

getting involved with any member of his team. Especially Blake Eastwood.

"Not particularly, but thanks for the idea," Blake said. "Picture this, itching powder and glitter." He tipped his head back and smiled, imagining the possibilities.

"How about you don't?" Valentina leaned past Cam, her gaze firm on Blake.

His head still back, Blake tilted his face."What about if I do that to an opposition player?"

"Still don't do it," she said before returning to her dough.

I liked her; she didn't have to say much to make her point, and the guys all listened and respected her. I wished I was more like her. She wasn't scared to take up space.

Me, the fact I chose the spot in the corner of the bakery said everything.

Blake shrugged, but didn't look deterred. Of course not, he probably had a full-blown plan in his brain already.

"Okay, place your loaves in your bowl to prove," Ian said. "That means it rises for the first time. Put them aside over there and we'll start the second group."

Everyone was quick to do as he asked, swapping

sides while the staff hurried about refilling the cups and changing out the sticky spoons for clean ones.

"How do I look?" Cam leaned over Nate's shoulder to look at the video on the defenseman's phone.

"Ugly as shit, as usual," Nate told him. "The best bit was when you ducked. The camera couldn't see your face." His eyes sparkled with humor.

"Fuck off," Cam said, shoving Nate with his elbow. "If I look bad, it's only because your camera skills suck."

Nate grinned. "I look forward to seeing you do better. Sorry, I meant *trying* to." He seemed very certain Cam would fail.

He might be right. My brother had a passing, casual relationship with his phone. He only used it to make a rare phone call, and text with Andi and the occasional group chat. I knew he had a team one and we had a family one as well. If it wasn't for that, he'd probably throw it away and not replace it.

Honestly, if he knew where and how to change photo mode to video, I'd be shocked. And if he did, I didn't want to know what he used it for.

"How much do you want to bet I can?" Cam asked. He stuck his chin out the same determined way he had since we were kids.

"I don't think they're hating this." I didn't notice Blake walking up to me until he spoke softly near my ear. "It was a good idea. They're going to spend all of these sessions trying to do better than each other."

Of course, they were professional athletes. They couldn't stop being competitive, even if their lives depended on it.

"Considering the mess, they might ban us from stepping foot in the place," I said.

Cleaning up after this was going to take a long time, even with the guys' help. I wouldn't be surprised if they made a bigger mess, all in the name of having fun. And by 'they,' I meant Blake. I suspected he wouldn't be happy unless we all walked out of here covered from head to toe in flour. Including himself.

In fact, I was surprised he wasn't wearing more of it after his turn making the dough. He only had specs of it here and there, except the clump still on his ear.

Blake chuckled. "It'd be worth it. The fans can laugh their asses off and the guys are bonding."

He gave me a long look like it wasn't the other guys he wanted to bond with, before moving away to rejoin them.

Chapter Six

Blake

"You brought that home to... Eat?" My roommate, Joe Santoro, pitcher for the Lowball Bay Sea Cucumbers, looked at my bread like it was something from outer space.

"What else would I do with it?" I asked. Just because it looked like something that came out the back end of a cow didn't mean it wasn't tasty. Right? I mean, it smelled good.

"You want some?" I pulled a knife out of the drawer and tried to cut into the crust. "It's a little harder than I thought." I pushed in harder. The knife snapped, the handle coming off in my hand. The blade remained embedded in the loaf.

Joe snorted. "If I knew it was that hard, I would

have taken it to work with me tomorrow. The team could always use a few extra balls."

I raised an eyebrow at him and grinned.

"Baseballs," he clarified. "We aren't short of the other kind." He actually pulled himself up a little taller.

"Mmmhmm, keep telling yourself that." I looked around for something to grab the blade with, so I could get it out of my bread.

"You're never going to cut into that," Joe told me as he stepped over to the fridge. "Save yourself some time and throw it in the trash."

"Where's your sense of adventure?" I asked.

"I left it out on the field after we lost the playoffs," he said.

"Interesting." I stroked my beard as if it helped me think. "So, what you're saying is that if you won, you would have, what? Gone bungee jumping? Eaten my bread?"

"I wouldn't call eating that adventurous." He eyed the loaf again. "I'd call that a death wish." He leaned over and tapped his knuckles on the crust. "I bet you've saved pucks softer than that."

"Hey, stop picking on Loafie." I turned the bread upside down, knocked the blade out with the handle and picked it up. Holding it in my palm, I pretended to stroke it like it was some kind of pet. "You'll hurt his feelings."

"Just when I think you can't get weirder, you get weirder," Joe said half under his breath.

I grinned. "No, this is about average." I stopped with my hand on the top of the bread and tapped it as he had. "You might be right, it is a bit hard."

"Don't," he said.

"Don't what?" I asked.

"Whatever you have in mind for that—" he waved his hand "—loafstrocity. Don't do it."

"What makes you think I have anything in mind?" I asked as I lowered the loaf to the floor and reached for a spoon with a long handle. As if it was a hockey stick and the bread was a puck, I hit it hard, making the loaf fly across the kitchen, into the cabinet on the other side. It hit with a thud and bounced off.

"If you damage this place, you're paying for it," Joe warned. "No way in the world insurance is going to believe you broke the kitchen with a piece of bread."

"If you're not careful, I'm going to start thinking you have a sense of humor." I stepped over to hit the bread the other way.

"Of course I have a sense of humor," he said. "I

share a place with you, don't I?" He opened the fridge and pulled out the ingredients for sushi.

"I thought that was because you had good taste in roomies," I said. I gave the bread a thwack, driving it up off the floor and hitting Joe right in the back of the thigh.

"Ow, fuck! Do you want me to sue your ass?" He rubbed the back of his leg.

"Sorry, bro." I scooped up the bread and reluctantly dropped it into the trash. "No lawyer would believe you anyway." I held the spoon up to my face like it was a microphone. "What did you say he hit you with? Bread?"

Joe shook his head at me and turned back to rolling sheets of seaweed. "I know why you're doing all of this."

I lowered the spoon. "All of what?"

"I saw that video of you pulling names out of your helmet. Now you're making bread. You're trying to impress that woman, aren't you? What's her name? Amanda? Amy? Veronica?"

"Her name is Alice," I said. "Where did you get Veronica from?"

"Don't deflect." He waved a sheet of seaweed at me. "I've seen the way you look when you mention her."

I leaned my back against the black marble counter top. "She hates my guts. She thinks I'm nothing but a menace."

Joe barked a laugh. "I wonder why she thinks that, Mr. Hit-bread-around-the-room? The same guy who put peanut butter and pickles on the sandwich just to see what it would taste like."

"It tasted good," I said.

Joe was one of the few people I didn't prank. I had to live with him. Having him irritated with me, or plotting revenge, made for uncomfortable roommates.

"My point is, stuff like that isn't for everyone," he said.

"I guess it isn't," I said with a sigh. "But I don't think that's it. I've seen her joke around with other people. She knows how to laugh. She just doesn't do it around me."

"Has it occurred to you that maybe she doesn't like you?" he said.

"I mean, it's possible," I said slowly. "I have been a pain in the ass to her where her job is concerned. After a few of the things I've done, she's had to do damage control. Like the time I ran one of the Humpbacks' jerseys up the flagpole."

Her face had turned red when she found out

what I'd done. She had to scramble to find an excuse for it. Some reason why it wasn't meant to be offensive. It wasn't, but people in Lowball Bay were as obsessive about their football as anywhere else in the country.

"I should have put Hawk Florence's boxers there instead." The quarterback was known for having a sense of humor. Sort of.

"And you wonder why she doesn't like you," Joe said. "You're making her work more difficult. Some PR folks have been fired for less. Every time you walk out the door, you're putting her job at risk. How would you feel?"

"I'm guessing 'entertained' isn't the right answer here?" I asked.

He gave me a look like he thought I was deliberately being dumb.

"Okay, so I like to take risks," I said. "I don't see what the big deal is. I wouldn't care if they ran a Sea Dragons jersey up the flagpole."

"You would if it was accompanied by the head of your mascot," Joe said. "How did you even get your hands on theirs?"

I smiled. "I'd forgotten about that. Also, I can't tell you. A magician never reveals their secrets."

"You're many things, but a magician isn't one of

them." He carefully sliced the sushi and arranged it on a plate with a lot more finesse than I ever possessed when it came to preparing food. His parents owned a restaurant, so I guessed it was in his DNA.

"Says you," I said. "Have you seen some of the saves I've made over the years? Don't tell me at least a couple of those weren't done with magic."

"Don't make me say they were done with skill." He waved the knife roughly in my direction.

I cocked my head and smiled. "Hey, Joe, how did I make those saves?" What can I say, I had an ego after all.

"You know what, it was probably luck," he said. "Or maybe the referee wasn't watching. Or you have a robotic extension in your catcher. It definitely ain't skill."

"Ouch, right in the feels," I complained. "I thought we were friends."

"We were friends, before you hit me with bread," he said. "Now we might be acquaintances."

He rolled his brown eyes at me, but he was clearly joking. At least, I thought he was. Joe held grudges, but only under the right circumstances. This wasn't one of them. Or I hoped it wasn't, because when he held a grudge, he clung to it like it was a life preserver. He once told me about Kevin Lovett, who stole his yellow crayon in first grade. If he met the guy now, he might punch him in the face.

"You know what I think," I said. "I think you're jealous you can't make bread as impressive as me."

"Yeah, I'm totally jealous of that," he said sarcastically. "I wish I could make bread harder than a baseball."

"At least you're big enough to admit it," I said, grinning.

He picked up a perfectly constructed sushi roll and threw it at me. Like any good pitcher, it came hard and fast. But, like any good goalie, I caught it before it hit me and popped it into my mouth.

"That's why we get on so well," I said, my mouth full of tuna, rice and seaweed. "You make good sushi."

"I should know better than to feed the animals," he said with a grunt. "They keep coming back for more."

I laughed and almost choked before I managed to swallow. "Yeah, I do."

I wanted Alice to come back to me for more. Joe was right: I wanted to impress her. I had to find a way to stop her from hating me first. Was that even possible?

"I should try to make bread like yours and see what happens," he said.

"I'd still keep coming back," I said. "My stuff is here."

"We could remedy that," he said. Joe ate a piece of sushi and nodded in appreciation. He waited until he swallowed to add, "We could run everything you own up a flagpole. Sticks, padding, underwear, everything."

"I'd be willing to let you try, if only to see if you could," I said. "I have a lot of stuff. At this point I should remind you the big screen TV is mine." I pointed in the general direction of the living room.

"I like a challenge as much as the next guy, but that could get someone killed," he said. "I guess I'm stuck with you. For now."

"Lucky you love me so much." I stepped forward, gave him a hug and a sloppy kiss on the cheek.

He waved me off and wiped the back of his hand down his stubble. "Don't push it. I have a date tonight. I don't want to turn up smelling like a goalie."

"She might like you more if you do," I pointed out. I raised my arm and sniffed my bicep. "I smell pretty good if you ask me."

"It's not me you have to impress," Joe said. "Maybe you don't smell good enough for Veronica."

I elbowed him in the side. "Her name is Alice. Alice North."

"That might be why she doesn't like you," he said, trying to hold back a smile. "Maybe she doesn't want to be Alice North-Eastwood."

I made a face at him. "If that was the real problem, I'd change my name. Blake North has a ring to it. And it would have the added bonus of confusing the hell out of the coaching staff. Hey, North. No, the other North!"

"You could always go with Eastwood-North, but it sounds like an affluent neighborhood." He popped another piece of sushi into his mouth.

"I like it," I said. "It sounds like a good place to put on the map."

And I was just the guy to figure out how.

Chapter Seven

Alice

"I don't think this is a good idea." I eyed Blake's ancient pickup truck. It looked like it had seen better decades. Was that rust on the front?

"It's a great idea," he said, flashing me a grin.

"Is this thing even road-worthy?" I asked.

That made him smile bigger. "I guess we're about to find out." He climbed into the driver's seat and turned on the engine. To my surprise, it actually turned over and started.

"See, nothing to it." He fastened his seatbelt.

"Just because it starts doesn't mean it's safe," I pointed out.

"Would I drive around in a dangerous vehicle?" he asked.

"Probably," I said flatly.

"I would not," he said. "And I wouldn't put you in any danger. Betsy here is perfectly roadworthy." He patted the steering wheel. "Trust me."

"That's exactly what I'd expect someone to say before they do something stupid," I said.

In spite of my better judgment, and maybe with an unhealthy dose of curiosity, I slid into the passenger seat and firmly clicked the seatbelt. That was working at least. I tested the 'oh shit' handle to make sure it was firmly attached in case I needed it. It was.

"You still haven't told me where we're going." He sent me a text telling me he had an idea for another challenge and that I was going to love it. I had my doubts, but after his bread making video went viral, I figured I could give him the benefit of the doubt.

Something I was seriously rethinking right now.

"You'll see. It's not far from here." He put the pickup into gear and pulled out onto the road in front of my apartment.

"If we're doing one of those eat-something-gross challenges, I'm out," I said. "I'm not eating cow eyeballs or bull testicles." I shuddered at the idea. I could be an adventurous eater when I wanted to, but not where things like that were concerned. Definitely not when I was being recorded.

"No, that's for next week," he said lightly. When I turned to glare at him, he laughed. "Okay, okay no gross food. Although, you might like the taste of testicles."

The wiggle of his eyebrows suggested he was not talking about animal balls. Of course he wasn't. And now I was thinking about his.

I pushed the thought away as hard as I could. I shouldn't think like that about any of the players, especially him. I was a professional. I had to have professional thoughts.

"We shouldn't be talking about testicles," I said tersely.

He grinned again. "Okay, but you were the one who brought them into the conversation," he said. "If that was what was on your mind, you know there's nothing wrong with that. Right?"

"It's not what was on my mind," I protested. "I just..." I shook my head. "Can we change the subject?"

"Sure. We can talk about dicks if you prefer?" He was teasing, trying to get a rise out of me. No pun intended.

"We're not talking about those either," I said. I wasn't thinking about his. No way. Except maybe kicking him there.

Whatever he was up to today, he better not be about to get me into a bunch of trouble. Who was I kidding? Trouble had a way of finding him, regardless. He was practically a magnet for it. And here I was, sitting in his pickup truck going who knew where, to do who knew what. I must be out of my mind.

"Penguins," he said.

I looked over at him and frowned. "Penguins?"

He glanced back for a moment. "Yes, penguins. I thought they might be a safe topic. Everyone loves penguins, right? When I was a kid, I wanted to be one. Imagine my disappointment when I realized it wasn't going to happen. But I walk like one sometimes."

I pictured little Blake waddling around his house, hoping he'd wake up the next morning black and white. I bet he was cute. No, I wasn't going to tell him that.

"I guess penguins are okay," I said with a shrug. "As creatures go, they're mostly harmless."

"See, that's what they want you to think," he said. "They act all cute and adorable, but you just know they're plotting world domination."

"Are you describing penguins or yourself?" I asked.

"You think I'm cute and adorable?" He stopped the pickup at a traffic light and smiled over at me.

"Those aren't words I'd used to describe you," I said. "I just thought you were projecting when you were talking about those penguins. And the bit about world domination."

"That part might be right," he said. He gestured to the floor in front of my feet, where a well worn notebook lay.

I leaned down to pick it up and read the hand written title on the front. "*The Goalie's Guide to World Domination?*"

"I like to jot down ideas in there," he said. "Who knows, maybe I'll publish it someday."

I looked over to him before I opened it to a random page about halfway in.

"Get all of the ducks on my side," I read out loud. "Ducks?" Did this guy have some kind of bird fetish?

"Ducks," he agreed. "Have you seen them when they get angry and territorial? You don't want the ducks pissed off with you. Or the geese. Or the pigeons; they might shit on your head." He seemed completely serious.

I turned to another page. "Be nice to the librarians. Don't tell me, angry librarians will throw books at people?"

"Probably," he agreed. "But mostly they know things. They're like penguins, they look innocent, but you know they know what you're thinking."

"Half of the book is empty." I flicked through a bunch of blank pages.

"It's a work in progress," he said.

"So I see." I put the notebook back beside my foot and looked out the window, trying to figure out where we were going.

"I think I should add an entry," he said. "Always be nice to PR people."

"That's a good general rule," I said. And surprising coming from someone who seemed to live by the expression 'no publicity is bad publicity.' Nothing seemed to be off-limits when it came to him.

"Here we are," he said, pulling up in front of an older stone building on Eel street. One of the first built in the city, it was at least a hundred years old. Surrounded by new buildings, it stood out like a grand old lady.

"Lowball Bay Ballet Academy?" I squinted at the name above the door.

"I wasn't always a hockey player," he said, climbing out of the pickup and coming around to open my door. "I figured you could film a practice session. I think it'd be good for young fans to see a player doing something like this."

I stared at him like I'd never seen him before. Maybe I hadn't.

"There might be a kid or two out there who wants to dance but is too scared to do it, because of what people would say," I said slowly.

"Exactly," he nodded. "I was that kid for a while. Then I realized life is too short not to chase your best dreams. So I danced and I played hockey, until I had to decide between them. I was never going to be a primo ballerino, so I chose hockey. But I still practice when I get the chance."

I'd seen him out on the ice twirling around, but I didn't know he was so serious about it. I assumed it was just Blake being Blake. Messing around because he could.

I must have been staring at him, because he shifted uncomfortably.

"If it's too out there, we can go and do something else," he said. "I don't want anyone to think—"

"It's a great idea," I admitted. "You're right, fans are going to love it." Okay, not all of them, but those who didn't could scroll past. The majority of the Sea Dragons' fans would love it.

"Great. Maybe I could film you doing some moves too." He started up the front steps at a trot.

"Don't push it," I said.

I was a band kid. Dancing was never an activity that interested me much. Honestly, the idea of getting up on stage and performing in front of other people was terrifying. I was happy to leave the performing to my brother. He loved the spotlight, no matter what he was doing.

Blake glanced over his shoulder at me and grinned. "Never say never. You might find you enjoy it." He pushed in through the front doors and held them open for me to follow him in.

The inside of the academy matched the outside's vintage features and character. Black and white tiled floors lead the way past timber door frames and the occasional brass chandelier, lights sparkling from them.

"I feel like I stepped back in time," I said in a reverent whisper.

"I feel like that every time I walk in here," he agreed. "It makes me wonder what the place was like when it was new. And all the things these walls have seen. If they could talk, they'd have a hell of a story to tell. Maybe even better than my world domination guide." His eyes shone with amusement.

No doubt the building had a lot more to say than 'be nice to ducks.'

"I didn't know you cared about old architecture," I said.

He shrugged one shoulder. "I think we should all care about history. Once it's gone, it's gone, y'know? Imagine all the people that have walked down these corridors. All the dancers and people coming to watch and... Whatever. The people who have made friends here. Fell in love."

His gaze dropped to my lips before he looked back into my eyes. "Imagine how many lives have changed here. Hundreds, maybe thousands. All the pirouettes, all the blood, sweat and tears. This old girl has seen so much." He patted the wall beside him.

"I guess she has." I stopped in front of a wall full of photographs, many black-and-white. Judging by the hairstyles, plenty of them dated back to the nineteen sixties and seventies. As far as I could tell, nothing was newer than the nineteen eighties. This wall alone held so much history.

"It's like a museum," I said.

In the corner of my eye, I caught him staring at me. I turned to face him. "What?"

He smiled slightly. "I wasn't sure if you'd get it.

Not everyone does. Some people like everything... I don't know, shiny and new. But you can feel how special this place is, right?"

"Yeah, I guess I can," I said softly. I liked shiny and new as well, but not *everything*. Something about building like this made me sad for the other old buildings torn down over the years. Some were too dilapidated to be repaired, but surely not all of them? Why were we always in such a hurry to get rid of our history? It was a shame.

"We should get on with your practice," I said, breaking the moment and letting reality crash back in. We weren't here to get nostalgic, we were here to work.

"Right, yes." He shook his head as if bringing himself back down to earth. "Walk this way." He gave me a grin before he pressed his arms close to his body, put out his hands and started to waddle like a penguin.

I shook my head at him. I wasn't going to walk that way, but I could follow him down the corridor.

Chapter Eight

Blake

I WIPED MY BROW WITH A TOWEL AND FINISHED my cool down stretches. This wasn't one of my longer practice sessions at the ballet academy, but I worked up a sweat with the exercise.

Or was it Alice's scrutiny during the entire thing? She held her phone in front of her face, but I watched her watching me. If I didn't know better, I'd think the interest was more than professional. Was that possible? I thought it was. Maybe she didn't realize it yet. If she did, she might have run away screaming. I'd have to work on her, but I'd do it carefully. The last thing I wanted was to scare her off.

"Did you get what you needed?" I asked. I spent some of the session clowning around, but mostly I was focused. There was a time to have fun and time to concentrate. If I was going to convince kids out there dancing was for them, I had to take it seriously. I won't lie, it was a struggle to keep a straight face with the phone on me, but I think I pulled it off. Neither my teacher nor Alice said otherwise.

"I think so," Alice said, her expression unreadable. She was tapping at her phone screen, watching the footage back. "I'll have to compile some bits and pieces, but it should do." She pushed her phone into her pocket.

"You're a tough crowd." I picked up the towel again and wiped the back of my neck.

"Sorry, I seem to have misplaced my standing ovation," she said dryly. "I'm sure it's around here somewhere."

I turned around slowly, my hands out.

"What are you doing?" she asked.

"Looking for it," I said. "Where did you see it last?"

She snorted. "The last time the Sea Dragons made the playoffs?"

"You really are a tough crowd," I teased. "I would have expected one each time I saved a goal."

"Of course you would," she said.

Silence fell for a few moments. I broke it with, "Is that a commentary on my ego?"

"Just stating a fact," she said. "Have you ever met a humble hockey player?"

I cocked my head and thought. "Now you mention it, no. To be fair, I've never met a humble professional athlete from any sport. I guess it comes with the territory. You've worked with a few, haven't you?"

"I've worked with my share," she agreed. "They're usually the ones who push the boundaries as hard as they can." She looked at me meaningfully.

"Some boundaries are meant to be pushed," I said, unflinching. "As long as I choose my boundaries carefully, where's the harm?"

"The harm is that you don't always choose right," she said. "You need to—"

Whatever she was about to say was interrupted as Linda, the owner of the Academy, bustled into the room before stopping suddenly.

"Blake! I didn't know you were here today." She looked troubled, distracted.

"It was an impromptu thing," I said. "Is something wrong?"

She held a piece of paper in her hand. What looked like an unfolded letter. She glanced down at it, clearly distressed at what she read there.

"Oh, I don't want to bother you," she said, forcing a smile.

"You'd never bother me." I stepped over to put an arm around her shoulders. "Come on, we've been friends for a long time. If something has you upset, I'm here to listen. Do Alice and I have to get shovels? You know, to help bury the bodies."

I glanced over to Alice, who looked unamused. Okay, what was new? I thought we made progress when she stepped into the building, but now...she was distant as ever.

Not that I was giving up. Not yet. No one ever said I was a quitter.

Linda sighed. "It's a letter from a developer. Another one. They want to buy the building and tear it down. I'm worried the city council will push for that. Some of them have connections to the developers. This place would make them a lot of money."

"They can't do that." Alice surprised me by speaking out before I did.

"What she said," I agreed. "This building is a part of Lowball Bay history." Tearing it down and replacing it with concrete and glass would be criminal. To do it so few people could make more money was disgusting.

Linda sniffed. "They might not give me any

choice. If the council decides it has to be torn down..." She shook her hair slowly.

"Then we fight," I said. "I'm not letting this place get imploded. Or exploded. Or any other kind of -ploded." I didn't care that wasn't a word, it was the intention that mattered.

"What can we do?" Linda looked defeated already.

"We'll do whatever we have to do," I said. "I can get the other guys on board. And the Sea Cucumbers. I bet the Humpbacks will want to help too."

"Blake," Alice said warningly. "The playoffs are coming. You're going to be busy playing, training and traveling."

"I'll squeeze it in instead of sleeping," I said.

"I don't think Coach Lampton will like that." She seemed conflicted. She didn't have the history with the building Linda and I did, but she obviously didn't want to see it destroyed either. On the other hand, keeping me on track on behalf of the team was literally her job.

"She's right," Linda said. "You're a busy man. You can't put your work to the side for one building. I'll figure out something." She closed her eyes and shook her head.

"I'm not letting you do this alone," I said. They

were right, I couldn't put my job aside, not this close to the playoffs. But I also wasn't letting this go. It was too important.

I looked over to Alice. "Don't tell me this wouldn't make good viewing. The guys getting behind a cause like this. People would eat it up."

"Yes, they would," she conceded. "But I'm going to have to run it past Andi and Coach Lampton first. They might not want you involved in something potentially controversial."

"Too late," I said flatly. "I'm involved. Besides, both of them would understand." I gave her a look, challenging her to disagree. Before she was the owner of the Sea Dragons, Andi worked for her father at Welling Development. She'd know what was at stake here for both sides. She'd know the right people to talk to to come to some kind compromise. Other buildings the developers could buy and work on.

Alice rubbed her temples with her thumb and fingers. "We won't have time for any more social media challenges."

"This is more important," I said.

"If it interferes with your job—" she started.

"It's going to cut into my pranking time," I said. "A lot of my teammates are going to go unpranked."

Okay, that made me slightly sad, but I had to pick my priorities. This was it. Right here.

On the upside, this gave me time to think up new pranks. And knowing they'd be looking over their shoulders, waiting for me to do something while I had nothing organized, was funny as hell. Almost as good as pulling an actual prank. It would drive them nuts and I was here for it.

Not to mention it would give me more things to write in my world domination notebook. Let them think I was plotting and planning in full view of all of them.

"Fewer pranks, what do you say?" I cocked my head at Alice and smiled.

"How about none?" she replied.

"How about none until the playoffs are over and this is sorted out?" No one said I wasn't willing to compromise once in a while.

Apparently that was the right thing to say, more or less, because she nodded. "Fine, but I'm going to help too. You're right, this place should be protected. Linda, have you filed for historical protection for the building?"

"I tried, I think that's what prompted this." She nodded down at the letter. "They're trying to get in before that can happen."

"Assholes," I said. "They must know it'll pass. I'm going to have to do what I do best. Defend the goal until full-time." The timing couldn't have been worse, with the playoffs looming, but we had to win. The academy and the Sea Dragons. There was no other option.

"Why do I think this is a bad idea?" Alice asked softly. "You could leave this to the experts. Talk to Andi and let her deal with it."

"Can you walk away now you've seen this building?" I asked bluntly. "Don't tell me you don't want to save it as much as I do. Because if you do say that, I know you'll be lying. I saw your face when you stepped through the door. You get it. You're not going to turn your back, and neither am I."

"I can't deny this place is special," she said. "But that doesn't mean this isn't a bad idea. Can you at least promise not to get into trouble over this?"

"No, but I can promise to *try*," I said. If we were going to win this, we might need to put ourselves out there more than we'd like. By that, I meant more than Alice would like. If that meant getting into trouble, so be it. If that happened, I'd handle it. Okay, she'd probably be the one handling it, but I'd help.

"Blake, I don't want you putting your reputation

on the line for this." Linda adjusted her tight bun, a sure sign of her anxiety.

"Actually, I think it'll be good for my reputation," I said. "For some reason, people seem to have the impression I do nothing but clown around." I worked hard to gain that exact reputation, thank you very much. Over the years, it served me well, but now it was time for a change of direction. A new game plan.

Alice snorted. "I wonder why."

I grinned. "No idea. There's more to me than practical jokes and catching pucks. Maybe it's time for people to see that."

And by people, I meant Alice. If this was what I had to do to impress her and save the building, then I'd go for it. I'd do this like I did everything in life, throwing all of myself into it, to hell with the consequences.

"You know I'm not a miracle worker, right?" Alice asked. "I mean, I can present all of this to the public, but they're going to think what they want to think. Especially if you continue to walk around like a penguin."

I pouted playfully. "Are you trying to clip my wings?"

"Penguins can't fly anyway," she pointed out. "But

if you want to show the world a different side of you, you're going to have to rein yourself in a little."

"That sounds boring," I said with a sigh.

"Then I guess we're done here." She took a step towards the door.

Like I was on the ice and she was a puck slapped towards the goal, I jumped to stop her, my hand on her shoulder.

"I can do this," I said firmly. "I'm not going to stop having fun, but I can show there's another side to me. Why does it have to be one or the other?"

"Because—" she started. She stopped and pressed her lips together. "Fine, I guess we can try this. But if it starts to go south, I'm pulling the pin. You'll have to leave this fight to other people." She looked at me firmly, eyes narrowed.

"Deal," I said without hesitation. "Did you mean what you said about me waddling like a penguin?"

"What do you think?" she asked.

"I guess I could do something different," I said. I flashed her a grin before stepping out of the room, walking like an Egyptian instead.

Her long sigh followed me out the door.

Chapter Nine

Alice

LIKE I SAID I WOULD, I SPOKE TO ANDI, WHO immediately called in the general manager, Justin Carmichael, and head coach, Brian Lampton.

"All the big guns," Rafe said, placing a tray of steaming mugs on the desk and handing out tea and coffee. "I had no idea that building was so important."

"Neither did I." I nodded my thanks for the coffee, but I was starting to think this whole thing was blown out of proportion. The scrutiny from the coach and GM had me wilting.

Should I have brought this to Andi in the first place? I could have told Blake no, couldn't I?

Who was I kidding? He would have gone ahead with it anyway. At least this way, we could keep the fire contained before it burned out of control. In theory.

"I thought the idea was to do a few quick challenges," the GM said. He lowered himself into a chair and sipped his coffee, his eyes sliding back and forth between me and Andi.

"That's what I thought," Coach said, looking less than impressed. "These boys have a busy few weeks ahead of them. This isn't the kind of distraction we need."

"No, but it seems to be the distraction we have," Andi said. "We all know what Blake Eastwood is like. Once he sets his mind to something, he's not going to stop no matter what we say."

"He'll back off if I tell him he'll be benched," Coach grumbled.

"You're not going to bench our star goalie right before playoffs," Justin pointed out. He turned to Andi. "Why are we here? Do we have a choice?"

"There's always a choice," she said. "If you're both adamant that he not be involved, we'll have to work something out with him."

I snorted softly.

Big mistake, they all turned to look at me.

"I'm sorry," I said quickly. "If you tell him no, he's going to go behind your backs. He's passionate about this. He's even agreed to stop pranking his teammates so he can focus on it."

"That would be the day," Coach said, clearly not buying it.

"You don't think he means it?" Andi leaned forward, resting her elbows on the desk.

"His middle name might as well be Prank," Coach said.

"I believe him," I said softly. I was putting myself on the line by saying that. If he proved me wrong, it'd be my ass in a sling.

"You really think it's that important to him?" Andi asked, directing the question to me.

Once again, I was the center of all the scrutiny.

"I really do," I said. "To be frank, I wouldn't have mentioned it to you if I didn't think it was. This has the potential to raise a lot of eyebrows, but fans love this stuff. Players with a cause."

I'd never admit it, but I found his passion both addictive and attractive. He'd have no trouble getting other people involved. He was probably downstairs right now recruiting the rest of the team. I suspected everyone in this room knew that. Deciding whether or not they'd allow it was a formality.

"I trust that, with Alice running point on this, it won't interfere with the team too much," Andi said.

"When it comes down to it, we can't dictate what the players do in their time off. They won't get much of it, so he's going to have to make the most of it."

"Personally, I like the idea," Justin said after an uncomfortable silence. "Think of it as team bonding. And the publicity is the kind you can't pay for. I might even take part myself."

"Me too," Andi said, resting her hand on her swollen belly. "I know that building. My father had his eye on it for years. It's prime real estate, but that's no reason to tear it down. In spite of what he taught me, there's more important things in life than money."

"What would they put there instead?" Justin asked.

She wrinkled her nose. "Probably an apartment building. The top few floors would have an incredible view of the city and the ocean."

"Doesn't sound too bad to me," Coach said. He held up his spare hand in surrender when Justin and Andi frowned at him. "I'm just saying, that's all. People need places to live."

"There's an empty block two streets back," Andi said. "It's twice the size. It's been sitting vacant for years. They could start there."

Coach shrugged. "It seems I'm outnumbered

anyway. Fine, as long as it doesn't interfere with training. At this time of season, rest is almost as important as working out. If you think this is a productive use of that time, then have at it, I guess." He pushed himself forward in his seat before standing. "I should get back to it."

Andi smiled and nodded. "Thank you, Brian."

I took that as my cue to stand as well. "If there's nothing else?" I asked.

"No, you're doing a great job." Andi smiled. "The team is lucky to have you."

"Thanks," I said awkwardly, stepping towards the door.

Before I closed it behind me, I heard Andi say, "So I hear you had an eventful adventure in the desert?"

I admit to being curious, but it was none of my business. I made sure the door was shut before I headed down to my office.

Like I always did these days, I checked above the door before I opened it farther and stepped inside. Lucky for me, no confetti fell on me. No paint or glitter either. In fact, nothing fell on me, but I almost stepped on a piece of paper that had been folded and pushed under the door.

Confused, I crouched to pick it up and open it. Words were hand-written on it with blue ink.

Dear Alice,

I'm leaving you this note because I'm too shy to say anything to you in person. The moment I saw you, I was captivated by your beautiful eyes and smile. You light up any room you step into. Whenever I see you, you make my day better. I just wanted you to know.

Sincerely, your secret admirer.

"What the fuck?" I asked myself. I looked up and down the corridor. Was anyone watching? They might have left the note and waited for my reaction. Maybe a prank from someone on the team. Of course, that was it. It was probably my brother thinking he was funny.

Asshole.

I crumpled the note in my hand and tossed it onto my desk. Why didn't I throw it straight in the trash? I don't know. Was there a chance it wasn't a joke? Someone else who worked in the team's front office could be interested in me. Right?

I flopped down in my chair and ran it through my head for a few moments. Who worked here that seemed shy? Honestly, a few of the staff were introverts. Myself included. They left being outgoing to those more inclined. Not just the players; a few others here were anything but shy.

Who did that leave? Leonard from accounts? He hardly said a word to anyone, but he was also twice my age. And wore lime green shoes with mismatched socks. Not that I was in a position to judge, but he wasn't my type.

I picked up the ball of paper, flattened it out, folded it and tucked it into my drawer. After all, it wasn't every day a girl got a letter from a secret admirer.

I opened my laptop and sent the footage from Blake's ballet practice to it, so I could edit it. The session lasted an hour and we only needed five or so minutes at the most. Trimming it down to the best bits would be difficult. Especially when he appeared on my screen, smiling as he went through warm up stretches, his movements fluid and strong.

Strength and conditioning was one of the most important areas players had to work on, and this workout was all of that and more.

He lifted his leg to place his ankle on the ballet

barre before leaning into a stretch. The muscles in his thighs bulged, and his ass was tighter than a drum.

I sat there staring at the screen for a few minutes before I realized I paused the video with him in that pose.

"Stop that," I told myself. I pressed play again and trimmed down the next section, where he went through the same stretch with the other leg. Not before stopping to wonder how it would feel to bite his ass. Or lick my way up his thighs. All the way up until I close my mouth around his—

"Alice."

I almost jumped out of my seat at the sound of his voice right behind me. Face hot, I swiveled around to see Blake himself leaning against the door frame, his arms crossed.

"I didn't mean to..." He leaned in, peering at the screen. "That's what had you so absorbed." He grinned slowly.

"I—" My voice betrayed me as I squeaked. "I was concentrating on getting rid of the unnecessary parts."

His grin got bigger. "That would be difficult. I don't have any unnecessary parts."

"I wasn't talking about your parts," I said as if I

wasn't just thinking about them. "I meant your practice session. We can't include all of it in the video. It'll be too long."

I didn't realize what I said until he raised an eyebrow at me.

"There's no such thing as too long," he said.

My eyes dipped below his waistband. He wore a pair of light grey track pants and you know what those are like. They did nothing to hide how big he was.

I swallowed and forced my eyes back up to his face. "When it comes to social media videos, there is," I said. "We don't want fans getting bored and scrolling on."

He placed a hand over his heart. "Ouch. Bored of watching me? Is that even possible?"

"Given the attention span of people these days, yes," I said dryly. Although, I'd sit and watch every minute of his practice if it was posted online. Then watch it again. And again.

What was wrong with me? I shouldn't be thinking about him, not like this. It was unprofessional and he was Blake. I reminded myself about the penis-shaped confetti, hoping that would get my thoughts back on track.

"Anyway, I spoke to Andi about your proposal to

save the Ballet Academy building." That was better. Thinking about the building made it easier to ignore the way my pulse throbbed between my legs. "She liked the idea."

"Of course she did," he said. "It's a good idea. The guys mostly agree. Those who don't..." He shrugged. "Who needs them?"

"I guess we can do without one or two," I said. It wouldn't help with team bonding, but as Andi pointed out, management couldn't dictate what players did in their own time.

"So I thought we could plan things out over dinner," he said.

I blinked at him, letting his suggestion sink in. "We're not going out on a date."

"Who said anything about a date?" He cocked his head.

"I—" Crap, he had me there. "I just wanted to be clear, that's all," I said.

Good save, I told myself.

"Crystal clear," he said. "I'll pick you up at six."

For a moment I thought about whoever wrote that note and what they'd think about this. Would they assume it was a date? They might be disappointed, presuming I was involved with the goalie. If that was the case, I might never know who wrote it. Should I tell Blake no?

When it came down to it, I didn't owe the letter writer anything. They could have approached me, but they didn't. Although, if they thought I was going out with Blake, that might encourage them to talk to me in person. Who knew where that might lead? Did I want it to lead anywhere? That was the question. I had no answer.

"Six sounds good," I said.

Chapter Ten

Blake

"I thought you said it's not a date," Joe said.

I looked up from where I was writing in my note-book to see him looking at me as if he didn't believe a word I told him. I quickly closed the notebook and put the cap on my pen.

"It's not," I said.

"Uh-huh." He took in my black pants and dark green button down shirt, best shoes and hair still wet from the shower. "You don't look like you're headed out for a friendly conversation." He sniffed. "You're even wearing cologne. Since when do you wear that?"

"Since I felt like it. Just because a guy goes to a bit of effort once in a while doesn't mean anything." Except it meant everything. This wasn't a date, but I wanted to impress her. If I had my way, it would absolutely be a date. With flowers and chocolates and everything.

I thought about getting those anyway, but decided against it. She'd give me the evil eye if I went that far.

Although, would a woman turn down chocolate? I decided that if anyone would, it would be Alice. No, better not to antagonize her. I'd have to win her over with my charm and good looks instead. Judging by the way she was watching the video, I was at least part of the way there. She was definitely ogling my ass and I was totally fine with it. I'd ogled hers more than once. Of course I had; her cheeks were perfectly round. I wanted to cup them and pull her to me, hold her there while I buried myself in her.

"You know what, you're full of shit," Joe said. "I don't think you believe what you're saying. I sure as hell don't. Especially since it's five o'clock and you're already ready."

He was right about that. As soon as I got home from the arena, I'd hit the shower and got dressed. I had so much time on my hands I'd sat down to write in my notebook. I would have left already, but I didn't want anyone thinking I was a stalker by sitting outside her apartment for an hour in my car, waiting.

Unless she was into that kind of thing. Yeah. I've seen the dark romance side of social media. Some girls went for the stalker type. Was Alice like that? Maybe. I might be missing an opportunity here.

"Better early than late," I said finally. "Alice isn't the sort of woman a guy should keep waiting. For one thing, she knows the passwords to my social media accounts." Which was one up on me, because I didn't have a clue.

"You think she'd post something inappropriate up there because you pissed her off?" Joe seemed to find that idea hilarious.

"Let's just say I'm not taking any chances," I said. "Speaking of chances..." I told him about the academy building and how we needed all the help we could get to save it.

He shrugged one shoulder. "I guess I'm in. The season is about to start, so I don't know how much time I'll have, but I'll give what I can. The other guys will probably show up from time to time too, but I can't speak for any of them."

"I'm sure you'll do your best to convince them," I said. "I'll speak to the Humpbacks too. At least those guys are in the off-season." I was friends with a couple of them, Hawk Florence and Bam Clinton. They were good guys. They'd want to pitch in, if only to have something to keep them busy before the season started again.

"If you're not careful, this thing is gonna take on a life of its own," Joe said. "Next thing you know, the whole city will turn out to protest, or whatever it is people do to save old buildings."

I smiled, imagining tens of thousands of people standing outside the front of the academy building chanting a catchy phrase and waving signs. Okay, I was getting a bit hopeful, but it could happen. Right?

"Did you just say I inspire people?" I teased.

"Absolutely not," he said. "I think I said old buildings inspire people. You just drew their attention to it."

"Uh-huh," I said slowly. "Keep telling yourself that. When this is over, they might rename the building in my honor. The Blake Eastwood building."

"More likely they'll put up a plaque," Joe said. "A really small one, low down on the wall where dogs can pee on it." He gestured down to his ankle.

"If you think that would upset me in some way, you're teasing the wrong guy," I said. "I'd love a plaque with my name on it, and I love dogs. Who wouldn't want them marking their territory on something with my name on it?"

"Just when I think you couldn't get weirder, you get weirder," he said. "No one else on the face of the planet would want that."

"I like to be different," I said. I opened my notebook and turned to the last page I'd written on. There, I made a note to be nicer to dogs. They'd be good allies if a guy was to attempt world domination. Which of course I wouldn't, but it gave me a laugh. What was life for if you couldn't chuckle a bunch of times a day? Or guffaw. Or even titter. I couldn't even think of the word titter without tittering. Could anyone? Now there was a challenge for my teammates. I made a note of that too.

"You succeed," Joe said as if he was insulting me in some way. "Shouldn't you be getting out of here?" He gestured up towards the clock on the wall, which was ticking the time away.

I glanced up. "Yeah, I should." I closed my notebook again and stood to toss it into my room. It landed on my bed, slid across the covers and off onto the floor on the other side. Which is a good indication of why I'm a goalie, not a baseball player. I could stop a puck like the badass hockey god I was, but my throwing could use some work.

Apparently Joe noticed and agreed, because he chuckled as he walked past. I decided to ignore him, because if he was handed a pair of ice skates and a catcher or a stick, he'd fall on his ass. Which, frankly, I'd like to see. Since we both knew what would happen, I doubted I'd have much chance of enticing him to try.

Spoilsport.

"Don't wait up," I told him. "Do you want me to bring you some leftovers?"

"I'm fine," he said. "Unlike you, I actually have a date tonight. No, you can't have the details."

I grabbed hold of the door frame and leaned out to look at him. "Nothing says suspicious like telling me you won't tell me anything."

"There's nothing suspicious about it, it's just none of your business," he said, heading for his room.

"It's someone I know, isn't it? Let me guess. Is it Valentina Ortiz? Or Chantelle Clinton, Bam's little sister? I know it's not my mother, she's not your type." She was also happily married to my father, but I couldn't resist the dig.

Joe barked a laugh. "As if I'd date your mom. She's probably weird like you."

"First of all, you met my mother and you know she's not as weird as me," I said.

He stopped, turned around to look at me.

I waited a few beats before grinning. "There is no number two."

He disappeared into his room, muttering something that sounded like, "Dickhead." He grumbled, but I knew he wasn't actually angry with me. At some point, he'd tell me who he was seeing, especially if it became serious. Hopefully before I stepped out of my room one morning to see a friend's little sister wearing one of his T-shirts. I should mentally prepare myself for that now, just in case.

I laughed and stepped over to look at my reflection in the mirror. Brown eyes, brown hair twisted in a neat man bun, freckles. My mother would call me cute. At least my hair wasn't a mess. And my shirt brought out the flecks of gold in my eyes. If Alice wasn't impressed by this, then... I'd keep working. One way or another I'd get her to stop hating me and thinking I was nothing but the thorn in her side. If I was lucky, we could be friends. If I was really lucky...

Okay, I was getting ahead of myself again. But her ass really was that perfect. Just thinking about it made me hard.

Down boy, I told myself.

'Myself' wasn't interested in listening. I had to think unsexy thoughts all the way down to my car. I didn't want to turn up at Alice's with a raging boner.

All right, I sort of did, so she'd know what she did to me. On the other hand, it might give her an easy target for her foot or knee, so flaccid was safer, for now. I promised myself I'd do my best, but I couldn't promise I'd succeed.

I just reached my car as my phone vibrated in my pocket. I pulled it out, glanced at the screen before tapping it and pressing it to my ear.

"Mom, were your ears burning?" I teased. "I was just talking about you."

"Nothing bad, I hope," she said.

"Of course not, I'd never say anything bad about you," I assured her. I didn't mention Joe. "Were you calling for a chat? Is everything okay?"

"Everything's fine," she said. "Your father is going out of town for a couple of weeks and I need a favor."

"I'm all ears," I said. "Except the bits that aren't ear. Which is actually a lot of me, now that I think about it." Since apparently there wasn't an emergency, I figured it was okay to joke around. I unlocked my car and slid inside before pulling the door shut behind me.

"Thank goodness for that," she said with a laugh. "I didn't think I gave birth to an ear. That would have been traumatizing to say the least."

Now I was picturing her imagining exactly that.

The doctor handing a crying ear to her, and her wondering what kind of bad dream she was living in. What can I say, us Eastwoods have vivid imaginations. It keeps life interesting.

Maybe, instead of writing about world domination, I should write a book about someone who gives birth to a baby which looks like a random body part. There would be a market for that, right? I mean, I'd read it. Especially if it became some strange, erotic romance. I could start a new trend. Ear smut. I made a mental note to think about that later.

It was my turn to laugh. Joe was right, she was as weird as me. In the best way possible, of course. I had to come from somewhere after all.

"I don't think I'd recover from it either," I said. I pushed the key into the ignition and started the engine. "What do you need?"

I listened as she spoke, nodding before she gave me the chance to respond.

"I'm happy to help."

"I knew I could rely on you," she said. "I love you, Blakey."

"I love you too, Mom," I said before I ended the call. By the sound of things, I wasn't going to have time to scratch myself for the next while. Luckily that suited me. I never could keep still.

Chapter Eleven

Alice

"I thought you said it's not a date," Vivian said, looking me up and down.

"It's definitely, one hundred percent not a date," I told her. "I just happened to be in the mood to wear a skirt and blouse tonight."

"Mmmhmmm," she said in disbelief. "Looks like a date to me. And you know what they say, if it looks like a date and it walks like a date, it's a date."

"I'm pretty sure they say that about ducks." I snatched up my bag from the hall table and pushed my phone inside.

"Ducks, dates, same thing," Vivian said with a shrug and a laugh.

"If you can't tell those two things apart, you might have a problem." I shrugged into a leather jacket and pushed my feet into boots before zipping them up. "I should be asking why you look all dressed up tonight."

She wore a long black skirt and a top that showed off her toned midriff, but the biggest indication was the massive hoop earrings she only wore for special occasions.

"I have a date-date," she said. "With a guy I met a couple of days ago."

"Whose social media profile should I be stalking?" I asked, only half-joking. I'd done it in the past and I'd totally do it again. What were friends for if we couldn't look out for each other?

"I already stalked it," she said. "He's legit."

"He better be." I gave her a quick hug, careful not to leave make-up on her clothes. "You know what to do if he's not."

"You too," she said. "Although, Blake Eastwood seems harmless enough."

"He's mostly only harmful to himself," I said dryly.

"It's the 'mostly' part I'm worried about," she said. "Don't wait up for me though, girl. And I won't wait up for you."

I returned her smile with a grimace. "I am *not* sleeping with Blake."

"You've thought about it," she said.

"I—" I shook my head. "I'm only human, okay, but it's not gonna happen. For so many reasons."

"Name three," she said.

"It's unprofessional," I said.

"The owner of the team is married to a player, and I know another player met his girlfriend at the arena," she said. "There's a precedent."

She was right, it was a thin excuse at best.

"It would complicate things," I said.

"It always does, but it's worth it," she said. "Unless he's really bad in bed. Is that what you're worried about? That he'd be terrible?" She gave me a sidelong look. "Or are you worried he's so good he'd ruin you for every other guy?"

I snorted. "Why are we having this conversation? I'm not sleeping with him. End of story. I should go. He's probably downstairs waiting for me." I picked up my bag and tucked it under my arm.

"He's not coming up here to pick you up?" Vivian asked.

"Of course not, because it's not a date," I said. "That's something a date would do."

"You want to know what I think?" she asked. Before I could say no, she continued, "I think you like this guy. You just won't admit it to yourself."

"He's a guy I work with," I said. "He's nice, but that's it. How many times have I come home from work complaining about him and the way he drives me up the wall?"

"Exactly," she said as though I made her point for her. "You talk about him more than you talk about anyone else. If that's not liking someone, I don't know what is."

I gaped at her for a moment before shutting my mouth in a snap of teeth. "It would never work out between us," I said finally. "We're too different. He likes being the center of attention. Everyone loves him. And me... I'm me."

"Alice North, you are one of the most amazing people I've ever met," Vivian said. "You're smart, thoughtful and sweet."

"Boring as fuck," I concluded. "It doesn't matter what I want, it wouldn't work."

"What do you want?" she asked gently.

I shook my head. "I don't know. I don't know what I want, okay?"

"Are you scared to take a chance in case you get hurt?" she asked.

"I mean, that's a part of it," I said. "Taking chances is...risky. Everything could go wrong."

"Everything could go *right*," she pointed out.

"When was the last time you took a chance? You know I love you to bits, but a risk-taker you are not. What would it hurt you to try?"

"Maybe it's not about me," I said. "If we try and things don't work out, Blake would be hurt too." I averted my gaze.

"He's a big boy," Vivian said. "He'd be okay." She seemed more worried about me than him, which was sweet of her. She'd always been such a good friend.

"Maybe he would. maybe he wouldn't," I said. "I don't take chances because someone always ends up regretting it. If it's not me, then it's someone else."

I sucked in a breath through my nose and blew it out through pursed lips. "I should get downstairs."

"Me too." She grabbed up her own bag and phone and followed me to the door. "You see, a date-date can meet in the foyer too."

"Does this guy have a name?" I asked.

"I've course he does. Would I date someone who doesn't have a name?" She looked cagey as we stepped into the elevator.

"If anyone would..." I said teasingly.

She nudged me with her elbow and laughed. "He totally has a name."

"What is it?" I asked.

"Look at that, we got all the way down to the first

floor without the elevator stopping," she said, clearly trying to dodge the question.

"Fine, I won't push you," I said with a sigh. "You'll tell me when you're ready." No doubt she had a good reason for wanting to keep it to herself. I knew it wasn't because he was my brother, so it must be something else. Maybe she thought I'd laugh if I knew. I wouldn't though, no matter who it was.

"Yes, I will," she agreed. "You'll be the third to know, after him and me."

"And everyone at... Wherever you're going tonight," I said. I peered through the glass doors that led outside to the street.

"Before you ask, I don't know where we're going," she said. "He said be ready to go somewhere nice."

Blake hadn't even said that much. Just that he'd take me somewhere where we could eat and talk about the academy building. Of course that was all he'd say because this wasn't a date. A small part of me envied Vivian, but I shoved it away. If this was a date, we might end up jumping out of a plane, or taking part in a hotdog eating contest. When it came to Blake, I couldn't begin to guess where we'd end up.

"Looks like he's not here yet," I said. "Your date, I mean." Blake was leaning against his pickup truck looking way too much like sex on legs for my own good.

"I see your date is waiting eagerly," Vivian said. "Go get him, girl."

"It's—" I started.

At the same time we both finished with, "Not a date."

"Good, I'm finally getting through to you," I said. I gave her a look before stepping over to the doors and pushing out onto the street.

My breath misted the frigid air as I hurried over to climb into the pickup truck.

"You look beautiful," Blake said, closing the door behind me.

I slid him a glance before he grinned and hurried around to the other side. That smile totally did not make my heart skip a beat. It was probably indigestion. From the meal I ate hours ago. My stomach rumbled, contradicting me like the traitor it was.

Whose side are you on? I asked it. The only response was for it to remind me I was hungry.

"Thanks," I said when he jumped into the driver's seat. "You look nice too." He looked better than nice. He looked good enough to eat. Starting with the bulge under his trousers.

I really needed to stop thinking like that or I was going to get myself into a world of trouble.

I swallowed carefully. "Where are we going?" That had to be a safe topic of conversation, right? Since this wasn't a date, there was no reason to keep it a secret.

"I was going to take you to Gianna's," he said, mentioning one of the most expensive and exclusive restaurants in the city. "Gianna managed to squeeze us in tonight."

"You were going to, but then?" I prompted.

I wasn't sure if I should be disappointed or relieved. I heard Gianna's was amazing, but it was the kind of place the rich and famous frequented. People like Jack Clutterbuck and Joe Santoro. And my brother, if I was honest. Not people like me. Although, I understood the food was incredible. It would have to be, for the price.

"Then there was a change of plan," Blake said. "I hope you don't mind, but I need to pick up an order of pizza, then... Well you'll see. Trust me?"

I gave him the side eye. "Haven't we had this conversation before?"

"Yes, we have," he agreed. "And I took you somewhere you liked, remember? So much so, you agreed to try to save the place."

"We're not going to chain ourselves to the big oak tree on Ballsac Street, are we? I know there's talk of cutting it down, but it's cold out."

"First of all, they better not cut the tree down," he said darkly. "But no, we're not going there. I think you'll like this. It's less flashy than Gianna's, and a lot warmer than a tree trunk."

"I feel like that's a weird clue to a cryptic cross-word answer," I said.

He laughed. "Can you think of anything warm, and thick like a tree trunk?"

Yes.

"No," I said. "Unless we're going to the zoo. The elephant enclosure fits the description." I gave myself a mental pat on the back for not thinking too much about his cock, and deflecting from what he was trying to suggest.

"We're not going to the zoo, but we can do that another day if you like," he said. "I have a season pass."

"Why does it not surprise me?" I asked. "Let me guess, your favorite is the monkey enclosure?"

He laughed. "Actually, my favorite is the penguin exhibit, but the monkeys are a close second. I have a season pass because the money goes to the breed and release program for the animals. They return as many of them to the wild as they can. The ones in the exhibits wouldn't survive."

It shouldn't surprise me he had a soft spot for animals, but it did. Most guys I knew didn't care. They were too busy worrying about their own careers to think about things like that. But Blake—it genuinely seemed important to him.

Animals, trees, history. Three things I wouldn't have thought the average goalie would even have on their radar. Or any other athlete, for that matter. Most of them were interested in one animal, the pussy, and getting as much of that as they could.

"So, if you ever go missing, I should find you chained to a penguin," I said.

He laughed. "Possibly. I mean, I have to look after them if they're going to help me with my plans for world domination."

"Of course you do." I shook my head at him. The more I got to know him, the more I realized there was more to him than just a jokester. That could be dangerous for both of us.

Especially my heart.

Chapter Twelve

Blake

The tang of garlic and tomato hit my nose the moment I pushed open the door to the pizzeria. Tuesdays were usually quiet. This was no exception.

Robbie stood behind the counter, his eyes down, tongue protruding as he carefully placed ingredients onto a disc of pizza dough. He stopped in the middle of placing pineapple, looked up at me and grinned with his whole face.

"Blakey! I can't leave yet, I have to finish this." He gestured towards the pizza with one of his small hands.

"Yeah, finish up, buddy," I told him. "Don't want you getting in trouble with the boss."

"Yeah, I don't want any trouble." Robbie grinned and went back to carefully placing the fruit.

"Why do I get the feeling he's been causing some?" I asked Donna, the owner of the pizzeria.

"It's in the Eastwood DNA?" she teased.

I pressed a hand to my chest. "Right there, right in the feels." I leaned backwards for added drama.

"Blakey, you're so full of shit!" Robbie declared.

Donna snorted.

I turned to Alice. "You see what I have to put up with? Called out by my own brother."

She looked from me to Robbie and back again. "I didn't know you had a brother."

I noticed she made no effort to stick up for me. Of course not, Robbie wasn't wrong.

"I try to keep him out of the public eye," I said. "You know how people are with people who are a little different. Robbie has Down syndrome, but that doesn't hold him back."

I didn't mean to get defensive, but I was protective of my little brother. Always had been, ever since bullies targeted him in school. He didn't let it get to him, but it got to me.

Alice looked at me funny, like I was a two-headed penguin.

"If you have a problem with my brother—" I started. I'd take her home right now and we'd be done. When it came to him, there was no bridge I wouldn't burn. Ever.

"Not at all," she said quickly. "You're not what I expected you to be."

I shrugged. "Yeah well... You too."

Cam had an ego the size of Lowball Bay, like the rest of us on the team. For some reason, I expected her to be the same.

She was the opposite. She wanted nothing to do with the limelight, fame or fortune. I was so used to arrogant hockey players and attention seeking puck bunnies, she was a refreshing change. Honest and real. Things I often wasn't, if I was honest with myself.

"Blakey, is that your girlfriend?" Robbie asked loudly. "Donna, Blakey has a girlfriend!" He laughed.

"She's not my girlfriend," I said. Yet. "She's just my...friend."

He went on laughing while he finished the pizza and carefully lifted it into the oven. He stepped back, just as carefully and went to the sink to wash his hands. He dried them with care, before hurrying around the edge of the counter and throwing his arms around me.

"What are you doing here?" He peered up at me

with his expressive eyes. While other people were closed books, he was always an open one. Whatever he was thinking was right there on his face. I wished more people were like him.

"I felt like pizza," I hugged him back. "Also, Mom asked me to give you a ride home. She got stuck with some work thing."

"Mom is always stuck with some work thing," Robbie complained. He unwound himself from me and stepped over to give Alice a squeeze.

She looked surprised, but after a moment she hugged him back. Of course she had more affection for my brother than she did for me. Figured.

"She gets busy, but it gives us time to hang out, right buddy?" I offered him a fist bump, which he returned with enthusiasm and force. "Hey, don't go breaking my hand." I shook it out and grinned while he laughed.

"What's your girlfriend's name?" he asked, peering at Alice.

"My brother has no filter," I said.

She smirked at me.

"Called out again," I said. "Okay, my brother, like me, has no filter. Robbie, this is Alice, she's Cam's sister. Alice, this is Robert James Eastwood, but everyone calls him Robbie."

"It's nice to meet you." Robbie gave her another hug. "Don't call me Robert. You're prettier than Cam."

"Everyone is prettier than Cam," I pointed out while Alice blushed.

"You're not," Robbie told me. His eyes sparkled with mischief.

"You're right, Robbie got the looks in our family," I said. "Just like Alice got the looks in hers."

"That's right," Robbie agreed, now pretending to be straight faced. "I'm the handsome one. Blake is the tall one. That's how they tell us apart."

Alice actually giggled. *Giggled.* I never would have picked her for a giggler.

"I'm glad you said that," she said. "Otherwise I never would have known which of you is which."

Robbie jabbed his elbow into my side. "Be careful or I'll steal your girlfriend."

"He'd do it too," I said, pretending to look sad. "My brother, the Casanova."

"Robbie, the pizza is ready," Donna called out.

His eyes widened and he hurried back behind the counter to take it out of the oven and place it in a box. That was followed by two more he must have put in before we arrived. He closed the boxes and piled them on top of each other.

"Let's go!" he declared.

I pulled out my phone to tap it and pay, adding a generous tip on top, of course. My brother was worth it; so was Donna for giving him a chance. So many other places wouldn't even try, but he was a hard worker and the customers loved him. It was a win-win for everyone.

"Thanks," Donna said, glancing at the screen. "Enjoy your night. Don't do anything I wouldn't do."

"How much does that leave?" I teased.

"You'll never know." She nodded at me and moved to serve a customer who walked through the door.

"My heart breaks again," I said with a dramatic sigh.

Her only response was to roll her eyes roughly in my direction and continue taking the order.

"Okay, let's get out of here," I said. I opened the door for Robbie who was carefully balancing the pile of boxes, his tongue protruding again as it did when he concentrated.

Once he walked past me, I said to Alice, "I hope you don't mind coming to my parents' place. It'll be quieter there than a restaurant anyway." Maybe I should have mentioned earlier that she'd meet my mother, but I was more worried about her response to Robbie.

"Quiet is good," she said. That was all she said before she stepped over to my car and climbed inside.

"Drive carefully!" Robbie called out from the back seat. "Don't get pizza on me."

"You could put them on the seat next to you," I suggested. "Then if I take a corner too fast, they'll only end up on the floor."

"Don't take a corner too fast," he said. "Right, Alice?"

"Right," she agreed. "What would your mother think if you brought home pizza that had been on the floor?"

I turned to raise my eyebrows at her. "If you think it would be the first time..."

It was her turn to roll her eyes at me. "My bad, I should have known. Do I want to know how many times?"

"Probably not." I started the engine and pulled away from the curb.

"Yuck," Robbie said. "I'm not eating pizza that was on the floor. I'm holding the pizza so it's not going to fall."

"Not all heroes were capes," Alice told him.

"I wear a cape sometimes," he said proudly. "Blakey and I go to comic con. Sometimes I dress up as Superman."

"Oh, really?" She looked over at me. "And what does Blake dress up as?"

I grinned.

"Let me guess, you cosplay as the Penguin?" she asked. "Or maybe just *a* penguin." She frowned before adding, "Don't tell me you go as Jason Voorhees?"

"I might have gone as all three of them," I said with an unapologetic shrug. "Not at the same time." What was the point of having multiple hockey masks if you couldn't wear one of them to a comic con? "Have you ever been to a convention like that?"

"A few," she said. "Before you ask, no I don't go as Alice in Wonderland." She'd clearly had people ask her that several times too many.

"You'd be cute like that," I said. "If you ever change your mind, I'd make an adorable Cheshire cat."

"I was thinking more along the lines of Mad Hatter," she said dryly.

Robbie laughed. "Blakey would make an amazing Mad Hatter. Let's do that next time! I can be... What can I be?"

"We'll think of something," I assured him. "Maybe we can coax Nate and Cam to come with us. They could be Tweedledum and Tweedledee."

Alice snorted a laugh. "I'd literally pay money to see my brother dressed up as Tweedledum."

"Me too," I said with a laugh. "Andi can be the Queen of Hearts. Although, that might be a better role for you." I could picture her with a tight fitting white dress and a huge red wig. Not to mention a croquet mallet in her hand, ready to play.

"I don't think it would be a good look for an employee of the Sea Dragons to walk around saying 'off with his head,'" she said.

"I know, I could be the rabbit," Robbie said. "I could get one of those pocket watches."

"My brother loves *Alice in Wonderland*," I said. "I think he's seen every version there is, a hundred times each. To be fair, I've watched them with him at least half of that."

My only regret at not living at home anymore was not seeing as much of my brother as I used to. Born a few years after me, we'd always been close. From the first moment I lay eyes on him, I'd been protective of him. Even if he wasn't atypical, I would have watched out for him. He was my brother, that's all I ever knew. All I ever cared about. He was different, but so was I. We embraced that and didn't let other people get us down.

"I stopped when people started teasing me about my name," Alice said quietly. She exhaled a long breath out her nose, clearly revisiting the past and feeling the weight of it, a burden she still carried around with her. No trauma stuck like childhood trauma.

"People can be assholes," I said. I wanted to hit everyone who ever bullied her, in the face with my hockey stick. If there was anything I couldn't stand in this world, it was a bully. Life was too short to be a shit human being, picking on the people around you.

"Yeah, they can," she agreed. "I ignored them and they eventually stopped."

"But it ruined your enjoyment of something that should be fun," I said. "That sucks. Maybe Robbie and I can help you with that."

An idea started to form in my brain. What was new? Something was always brewing in there, good or bad. Sometimes they saw the light of day, often not.

In spite of what some people might think, I actually had a small measure of common sense. Okay, laugh at that, but it's true. I knew where to draw the line. Sometimes I even stopped before I crossed it.

She gave me a questioning look, but I didn't say anything else. Instead I focussed on driving carefully to get home safely with the pizzas, and two people I was starting to care about more and more. If I wasn't careful, I'd fall for this woman, hook, line and sinker. Okay, skates, padding and all.

Chapter Thirteen

Alice

"This is Alice, she's Blakey's girlfriend," Robbie declared as he carried the pizzas into the small brick house.

Blake glanced over at me and shrugged. "He's stubborn when he gets a thing into his head."

"I can tell," I said. It must run in the family. "He's sweet."

"He has his moments," Blake agreed. He gestured for me to step into the kitchen before him.

"Blakey has a girlfriend?" The woman who was pulling plates out of the kitchen cabinet could only have been their mother. She had the same dark hair, dark eyes and freckles. Her mouth was wide, and her eyes lined with laugh lines, suggesting she had a sense of humor like her sons.

"We're just friends," I said. "I'm Alice North."

"Marilyn Eastwood..." She seemed disappointed, but held out her hand for me to shake. "North, as in..."

"Cam's sister," I finished for her. Sometimes I thought I should change my name to exactly that, since so many people referred to me that way. And saw me that way. As if I didn't have an identity of my own. I doubted he'd ever been referred to as 'Alice's brother' in his entire life. Of course not, he was the one everyone noticed first. And since he became a famous hockey player, I was a distant appendage.

"He's been here a few times," Marilyn said. "He seems nice."

"Yeah, he always gives that first impression," Blake said. "Then people get to know him and see the real Cam." He took the plates from his mother and spread them out on the island while Robbie opened the pizza boxes carefully, inspecting them for damage.

"I'm sure they say the same about you," Marilyn said.

"Nope, I'm always nice." Blake picked up a piece of mushroom and popped it into his mouth.

"Ha ha, that's funny," Robbie said. "Blakey is always nice." He jabbed his elbow into Blake.

Blake huffed. "I didn't come here to have all of you pile onto me." His eyes shone with humor.

"Are you sure?" Marilyn asked.

"I was, but now I'm not." He cocked his head to the side before surrendering to a smile. "You're right, I came here for the pizza. Mmm, delicious carbohydrates."

He snagged a couple of pieces and placed them on a plate before opening the fridge and taking out a couple of beers. He glanced at me questioningly. When I nodded, he pulled out a third, handing one to his mother and one to me before opening his.

"I hope you don't mind casual dining." He nodded towards the living room before carrying his food and drink inside and flopping down on a chair.

"It's fine," I said.

My parents had always insisted we sit in the dining room and talk about our day. That usually consisted of Cam talking about his day while I ate quietly. Usually as quickly as I could, so I could go back to my room and whatever book I was reading at the time. The ritual was nice, but this was a pleasant change. No pressure to keep track of a conversation you were barely paying attention to.

I sat down beside Blake while Robbie sat in an

armchair. Marilyn took her meal and disappeared into what I assumed was her office.

Blake gave me a glance before reaching for the TV remote and turning it on. The screen itself was enormous, almost taking up an entire wall.

"It's okay if you don't want to," he started, stopping the remote on the icon for Alice in Wonderland.

I was certain he'd put on something else if I asked him to, but he and Robbie both looked so hopeful, what could I do but nod and bite into my pizza? The food was delicious and I could sit through one viewing, right?

"Go ahead," I said once I swallowed.

"Tell me if you change your mind," Blake said. "We can always watch something else. I have about eleven million replays of Sea Dragons games on here."

I arched an eyebrow at him. "Only eleven million? Where are the other twelve?"

Cam probably had at least that many. I doubted he watched them, I had to give him that, but he kept them. No doubt he'd be showing them all to his and Andi's kids some day.

"He accidentally recorded over them with porn," Robbie said, looking gleeful at his own burn.

Blake turned to him for a moment, then burst out laughing. "Don't listen to him, it was Robbie who recorded over them with replays of baseball games."

"Baseball is far superior to hockey," Robbie declared. "I can play baseball." He pulled himself up proudly.

"I think Robbie likes my roommate more than he likes me," Blake said.

"Joe is cool." Robbie nodded. "He's the best pitcher in the history of the Sea Cucumbers. And he said I'm the best hitter they never had. They should put me on the team. I'd get all the home runs."

"Joe coaches the team with disabilities," Blake said. "Some of them would give the pros a run for their money." He looked wistful for a moment, with a hint of frustration because that would never happen, but covered his face with his bottle before taking a sip of beer.

"I bet you're better at playing baseball than I am," I said. "I can't hit a ball if my life depended on it."

"I'll tell you a secret." Robbie leaned closer and cupped his hand around the side of his mouth. Loudly, he said, "I can't ice skate. I tried, but I kept falling on my butt."

I smiled. "I can ice skate, but not well. Better

than I can hit a ball. Or throw one, for that matter. But I can play the saxophone. And the clarinet."

Robbie's eyes widened. "You're so cool! Only cool people can play the saxophone, right Blakey?"

"Exactly," Blake said. "I was going to try to learn when I was a kid, but realized I'm not cool enough." He didn't seem too worried about the fact. Of course not, no one would accuse him of not being cool enough to play a musical instrument. No one but himself.

I added his brother to that short list when Robbie said, "Yeah, Blakey is not cool." He laughed, then added, "I'm kidding. My brother is the coolest. One time, a guy at school was being mean to me and Blakey hit himself in the face with a cupcake. It was so funny. You should have been there."

I raised my eyebrows at Blake again.

He shrugged. "It seemed like a good idea at the time. He stopped teasing Robbie and laughed at me instead."

"Was that why you did it?" I asked softly. "So they'd leave him alone?"

For once, Blake looked serious. "I guess so. Or maybe I wanted the attention."

"I don't believe that," I said. He wasn't the kind of guy who diverted attention from his brother just to get it for himself. If he did it, he did it for a reason.

He averted his gaze. "Yeah, well. It's what anyone would do, right?" He swallowed hard, his Adam's apple bobbing up and down slowly, visible under the hair of his beard.

It wasn't something my brother would do, or anyone else I knew. Cam had his protective side, but he wouldn't clown around so people left me alone. He'd be more likely to take a swing at them.

Although, he'd never needed to divert attention from me. He could do that just by entering a room. Ten seconds later, bam, Alice who? Sometimes I felt like I might as well have ceased to exist. Which was fine with me. I preferred to blend in with the background. It was a lot less pressure than standing in center stage.

I took a sip of beer. This conversation and line of thought were getting heavy and bringing down the mood. Now would be a good time to let it go for a while. To take a leaf out of Blake's book. Not the world domination one, the one where he cracked jokes to make people smile.

"What flavor was it?" I asked. "The cupcake, I mean."

"My favorite, lemon," Blake said. He seemed

relieved to change the subject. Or at least, lighten the moment.

"Lemon is good," I agreed. If we kept talking about them, I was going to have a craving for them. I couldn't remember the last time I had a lemon cupcake. Or a cupcake of any kind.

He looked at me in surprise. "I don't think I've ever met anyone who liked them too. People usually prefer chocolate."

"I like that too," I said. "I mean, it's cupcakes. What's not to like?"

"Right," he said. "They are pretty awesome."

I leaned against the back of the couch and finished my pizza while watching the movie. Every so often, I'd glance over to Blake. He was pretending he was engaged with the movie, but every time I looked at him, his face snapped away as though he'd been staring at me instead.

I thought about calling him out, but what would I say? Chances were, he wouldn't admit it, otherwise why look away every time? No, better not to ask.

When we finished eating, he took both of our plates and returned them to the kitchen before coming back with another beer and a glass of water. Beer for me, water for him.

"We should be working on that plan," I said.

"We can do that after the movie," he said. He draped his arm over the back of the couch, behind me.

He made no move to touch me, but I was all too aware of how close he was. Warmth radiated from him, and the masculine smell that was purely Blake. A smell I tried hard not to inhale too deeply, in case I became intoxicated on it. Smelling like that should be illegal.

I resisted the urge to nestle up closer to him. This was not a date and he was not my boyfriend. Him letting me see a whole new side to him didn't change anything. He was still the guy who joked around and caused trouble. So what if he had a softer side? The seriousness wouldn't last, especially when we were in public or he was around his team.

Honestly, I didn't want it to. Blake without the laughter wouldn't be Blake. I wasn't the kind of woman who thought she could change another person. To make them what she thought they should be.

I accepted people as they were. No more and no less. Wild side and all.

That, right there, was another reason we couldn't be together. I'd always worry about what he'd get into next and if he'd get hurt. At some point, I'd inadvertently shackle that side of him. He'd see me worry and decide to dial it back. That would only lead him to resent me.

Resentment had no place in a healthy relationship. It makes everyone involved miserable. No, it was better to stick to being friends and ignore my growing attraction to him.

Maybe it was better that we not be friends at all. I shouldn't have agreed to come here tonight. I didn't want to give him the wrong idea. He deserved better than that.

And yet, I couldn't remember a time when I was more relaxed than I was right then. Blake saw me. Me, Alice North, not his teammate's sister. He invited me into his home, introduced me to his family. Let me understand more about him and his brother.

I had a feeling he didn't do that for just anyone. His joking around wasn't only to protect his brother when they were kids, it was to keep the attention from him now. So Robbie could live his life without scrutiny. If everyone was looking at Blake, no one was looking at Robbie except people who were supposed to.

Do not fall for him, I told myself.

Except it might be too late for that.

Chapter Fourteen

Blake

Robbie disappeared into his room after we finished the movie and Mom disappeared into hers. That left Alice and I alone to clear up the plates after dinner and sit down to discuss the plan to save the academy building.

"Why PR?" I asked while she wrote down notes in her neat handwriting.

She glanced up at me. "I don't know. I suppose because I spent a lifetime watching people react to other people. I kept thinking if they did this instead of that, then things would be different."

"So you decided to help them do this?" I said. "And teach them not to do that."

"Something like that." She looked back down. "Some of them even listen."

"Ouch," I said without any heat.

She put down her pen and rested her elbows on the table. "Don't tell me you listen. That would mean you ignore me willfully."

I slid my gaze sideways. "It's not like I *want* to ignore you when you tell me not to do things."

"But you do it anyway," she said. "I feel like if I told you not to hit yourself in the face with a cupcake, you'd hit yourself with two of them."

"I would not," I protested, looking back at her. "I..."

"Let me guess," she said slowly. "You'd hit one of your teammates in the face with them instead."

I grinned. "I like that idea. A couple of them could do with some loosening up." I snatched up my notebook which sat on the corner of the table and scribbled on a new page.

She groaned. "I shouldn't give you ideas."

Her groan was certainly giving me ideas. And reminding me we were alone in the living room. Neither my mother nor Robbie would show their faces until morning. Although, they'd hear her scream. And she would scream when I touched her. I'd make sure of that.

"Don't tell me you don't want to see Cam's face

covered in cupcake," I said. "Or Nate. I know he's given you some challenges in the past."

"'In the past' being the key words," she said. "You're more like past, present and future."

"You think we have a future?" I asked. Why not cut right to the chase? I knew something was happening between us. It was only a matter of time before things escalated. Unless I was reading the room wrong, but I knew I wasn't. I drove her up the wall, but she was starting to like me.

"No." She picked up her pen and started writing again.

I grabbed the pen out of her hand and held it over my shoulder, out of reach. "Why not? You like me, I like you. We have things in common. You don't hate *Alice in Wonderland* anymore."

"You can't base a relationship on not hating a movie," she said. She held out her hand for the pen.

I didn't give it to her. "There's more to it than that. What's holding you back?"

She responded with a long sigh and ran a hand over the back of her hair. It was just long enough to wrap around my fist. I wanted to do that right now. To kiss her. To taste her. To get her to admit how she was feeling.

"I don't date hockey players," she said finally.

"I know some of us can be dicks," I said. "You're not lumping us all in together, are you?" I frowned. "You are, aren't you? Is it because of your brother? You're worried you'll end up with someone like him? Apart from playing hockey, he and I are nothing alike. I'm not grumpy, for one thing."

"He'd be grumpy if he knew we were having this conversation," she said. "But no, it's nothing to do with him. It's a once bitten, twice shy thing."

"A hockey player bit you?" I asked, pretending to take her words literally. That could have been what happened. Some of us were known for being feisty. And her ass looked good enough to sink my teeth into.

She snorted. "You could say that." She looked down toward the table. "Do you remember Kyle Parkinson?"

I thought for a moment. "Yeah, I do. He was a winger for the Mackerels." A lot of junior players got their start there, before being drafted to the NHL.

"He was ambitious as fuck until he got injured out," I added slowly. "He's working as an equipment manager now." I'd seen him around the arena a couple of times lately, but hadn't given it much thought. Shame, he had a lot of potential.

"He was injured when he overdid his training," Alice said.

"So you won't date another hockey player because you think they'll be the kind of guy who won't listen when they're told not to go too far," I said. If that was the case, she was definitely describing me. That would explain her reluctance.

"That's part of it, yes," she agreed. "But he also looked up to my brother."

"Cam is tall," I deadpanned.

She gave me a sideways evil eye, which I totally deserved.

"So, he respected your brother," I said.

"Cam was already playing for the Sea Dragons when Kyle and I were seeing each other," she said. "Kyle idolized him. He wanted to be just like him. Whenever Cam was around, I ceased to exist. Eventually I realized he was only dating me so he could spend time with my brother. Kyle thought they could be friends, or that maybe my brother could help his career. As if Cam had any say over who was chosen for the team."

"Kyle was using you to get to your brother," I concluded. I lowered my hand and dropped the pen to the table with a clatter.

"Exactly," she said. She toyed with a small silver

ring on her right hand. "Looking back, it was so obvious, but I didn't see what was right in front of me. I was so used to Cam being noticed that I didn't even think anything of it. It was...normal."

"Kyle is an idiot," I declared. "No offense to Cam, but anyone who can't see you past him needs to get their eyes checked."

When she was in a room, she was all I saw. All I wanted to see. The rest of the world could take care of itself. It disappeared when I was with her. If it ceased to exist when we were together, I might not even notice.

"You know I'm not sitting here with you right now to get your brother's attention, right?" I asked.

"If I'm involved in saving the academy building, then he's likely to get involved," she said softly. "There's more chance we'll be successful with more people involved. Especially someone as high-profile as he is. And with him comes Andi."

I put one of my hands over hers. Her skin was soft and warm under my palm. A jolt of electricity shot through my palm, all the way down to my balls.

Not now, I told them. They weren't happy about it, but they'd wait. After all the ways I risked them over the years, at least this was safe. Honestly, it was a miracle I hadn't at least lost one testicle by now.

Okay, give it time; it could still happen.

"If it's just us, doing this, that would be fine with me," I said. "You and I can take on this fight together. Between the two of us, we can win this. If other people come on board, then great. But I'm not spending time with you because you might help encourage other people to get involved in this fight. I want to spend time with you."

"Having other people behind us will help," she said. She was right, it would, but that wasn't the point right now.

I shrugged. "I guess so, but..." I looked right into her beautiful eyes. I'd never seen that shade of blue anywhere else in my life. I couldn't even compare it to anything. The closest I could come was the deepest part of the ocean. I could have drowned in them then and there.

"Alice North, I'm not using you to save a building. I'm not using you to get to anyone. This isn't even about trying to get my reputation back on track. I like you. That's all."

She stared back at me, not saying anything. Maybe not believing a word.

I couldn't tell what she was thinking, but my heart raced as I leaned forward and lightly pressed my lips to hers. She tasted like beer and pizza, and something uniquely her.

Immediately, I wanted more.

"Blake," she whispered.

Then my hand was on the back of her head, kissing her, devouring her. My tongue slid between her lips, tangling with hers and tasting the inside of her mouth. And by some miracle, she was kissing me back.

"We shouldn't," she said, pulling back.

"Why not?" I whispered. I knew she wasn't telling me she didn't want to. The press of her lips against mine told a different story.

"You want me to make a list?" she whispered back.

"A list would be good," I said jokingly. I ran the pad of my thumb down her neck and over her throat. Then the rest of my hand, lightly circling her throat and feeling her pulse jump under my fingers. How would it feel to hold her like this while driving into her? I'd bet anything she'd feel like heaven.

I wanted to find out, badly. But tonight was not the night. When I made her mine, she'd have to know I meant it. That it wasn't some game or joke for me.

"My brother might kill you." She didn't pull

away. If anything, she leaned into my hand. Her eyes were dark, but wary. She wanted me to, but she wasn't going to jump in. Not yet.

"He won't kill me," I said. "He's not a complete Neanderthal." Close, but not completely there. "He'd tear me a new one if I hurt you, because he's protective of you, but he wants you to be happy." And if he didn't, he was an asshole, because her happiness was more important than anything. Besides, if I was good enough to be his friend and teammate, then I must be good enough for his sister, right?

"Are you worried about what he'll think?" I asked.

"No," she said. "Okay, *yes*. He doesn't think you take anything seriously. He's going to assume you won't take me seriously either. He'll be sure you're about to break my heart at any moment."

"Then we'll have to show him otherwise," I said. "Because I take you very seriously. More seriously than I've taken anything for a long time." I stroked my fingers over her pulse point, enjoying the way she shivered in response.

"But how long will that last?" she asked. "Until something more fun comes along?"

"What could be more fun?" I asked. "Or more

beautiful? Or smarter?" I was starting to understand her. She spent her life in her brother's shadow, trying to make herself as small as she could so she wouldn't get in the way. No wonder she hated the spotlight. She kept out of it out of habit. Because she was so sure no one wanted to look at her anyway.

She was so wrong. She deserved center stage. She deserved to be the main character of her life and her story. And I was going to make it my mission to do that for her. As long as she'd let me.

I pressed my forehead against hers. "Give me a chance, that's all I ask. Give me a chance to prove this can work. All you need to do is say yes."

A long silence fell. I thought she wasn't going to respond but then she whispered so softly I almost missed it.

"Yes."

Chapter Fifteen

Alice

I held my phone up in front of me and filmed the team skating back and forth across the ice, warming up. Blake was over near the goal, casually skating backwards, in circles, while writing in his notebook. He seemed to have it with him all the time these days. If that was his outlet instead of pulling pranks, then I was all for it. Honestly, I was still waiting for him to pull something, but as far as I knew he hadn't yet.

"Things have been a bit quieter around here lately," Valentina said, stepping over beside me. She wore a tracksuit in team colors, her hair pulled back in a neat ponytail.

"They're focused on training for the playoffs," I said, glancing over to her.

"That's part of it, yes," she said. "Okay, a big part of it. They might just pull it off this year and win the Stanley cup."

"They're on form," I agreed. I followed my brother and Nate as they chased a puck down the ice, hitting it back and forth between them. They made it look effortless, but I knew it was a lot more difficult than it seemed.

Cam turned and slapped the puck to Flynn, who intercepted it before slapping it back.

"I wouldn't have even seen that coming," I said.

"Everyone has to be ready for anything like that to happen at any moment," she said, her voice tight.

I glanced over to her again. "Of course, I just meant... Nevermind."

"I'm sorry," she said. "The playoffs are a lot of pressure. Their first game is only a couple of days away. It's...intense."

I turned off the recording and lowered my phone. I had enough footage of today's training to put up a reel or two.

"Because this is your first season as an assistant coach in the NHL," I said, half asking but mostly stating.

"Yep," she said simply. "There's people out there hoping I'll fail."

I snorted softly. "Of course there are. Because if the team loses, it's all the fault of a woman."

I'd seen the comments on social media. Usually along the lines of her being there to make sandwiches for the guys, or that she should go back to the PWHL. Some even suggested she was there because she was sleeping with Brian Lampton, which was laughable at best. At worst, it was disgusting. She was here because she deserved to be here.

She shrugged. "I try not to let it get to me. I know I'm inspiring girls all over the continent. Girls who wouldn't try to play hockey otherwise. One day soon, we'll be on even pegging with the men."

I grinned. "That'll teach them. Personally, I think what you're doing is awesome." I'd gone along to film some of the events she'd been a part of. The girls adored her. The guys adored her, too. It was only the keyboard warriors and a handful of clueless fans who thought otherwise.

"Same to you," she said. "You've done good things for the team. Making bread was fun, and watching the videos and reading the comments was hilarious. I hope Blake didn't try to eat his."

"It wouldn't surprise me if it's sitting on a shelf at his place," I said, half-joking again.

"You know, that wouldn't surprise me either," she

said with a smile. "He's one of a kind, even amongst goalies." That was saying a lot, given how energetic and unique many of them were.

"It takes a special kind of person to stand in front of a puck when it's coming at you at a hundred miles an hour," I said. Even with all the padding, and helmet they could get hurt. Not to mention the wear and tear on their bodies from kneeling and diving.

And then there were the groin stretches. Which Blake was doing on the ice right now. He put his notebook away and was on his hands and knees, moving back and forth slowly as though he was driving into an invisible partner. As if he was driving into me while I lay there underneath him, slow and deliberate. His hand wrapped around my neck like he'd done the other night. Hitting me deep inside, making me groan and scream. His breath ragged as he thrust and thrust, increasing the friction until we both came...

"And they wonder why hockey romance books are popular," Valentina said. She wasn't watching him, she was watching my reaction to his stretches.

My face heated and I swallowed hard, carefully averting my gaze from him. "It is something to witness." I'd seen it plenty of times before, but it never affected me like it did now. My panties were officially ruined.

Valentina chuckled. "I suppose it is." She looked out at the ice. Her gaze was tracking Flynn's movements as he called out encouragement to the other players and finished his own warm up. Her eyes seemed to grow as cold as the rink.

"Is something going on between you and Flynn?" I asked gently. Clearly something was, but I had no idea what.

She grunted a breath. "What makes you think that?"

"I get the impression you don't like each other," I said. Of course, not everyone got along, but their animosity seemed to be something more. Like they'd both be happy if the other one went away and never came back.

"He doesn't want me here," she said finally.

I frowned. "Because you're a woman? He doesn't seem the type to—"

We were interrupted by one of the office staff calling out my name.

"Alice! There's a delivery for you."

I shot Valentina an apologetic glance before heading over and taking the box from the young intern. I nodded my thanks before he turned and slipped back through the doorway.

I glanced over to Blake, who was looking in my direction. His mask hid most of his expression. If this was from him, I couldn't tell. But who else would be from?

I teased open the lid and stared at the six perfectly round, beautifully decorated yellow cupcakes. I leaned in to take a sniff.

"Lemon." My stomach rumbled at the smell. A small part of me wondered if they were full of laxatives, but I decided they probably weren't.

"Someone has a fan," Valentina said.

I looked back to the ice to see Blake skating over toward us.

He pulled up his mask and frowned. "You ordered lemon cupcakes?"

"No, they were just delivered," I said. "You didn't send them?"

He shook his head. "I wish I had. Is there a name in there?" He looked genuinely irritated, as though annoyed at the idea someone else would send me cupcakes.

I'd never seen him jealous before. I wasn't sure what to make of it. Had someone sent me these to make trouble? If they had, how did they know? We'd agreed to give each other a chance, but that was it. Nothing official, and we hadn't said anything to anyone yet. This was all too new for someone to try to mess with. Wasn't it?

I peeked into the box before raising it to look underneath and turning it around to glance at the sides.

"Nothing." I thought back to the note that was slipped under my office door. The one that said it was from my secret admirer. I hadn't recognized the handwriting, and I hadn't realized until now I assumed Blake sent it. He could have asked someone else to write it. He wasn't short of notepaper, since he carried his notebook around so much.

But if it wasn't from Blake, who was it from? Or was the note from Blake and this was from someone else?

I lowered the box and looked over in Cam's direction. Had he done this? I couldn't remember him ever having sent me anything before. If he was behind this and the note, then he was fucking with me for some reason. If that was the case, he might end up with me kicking him hard in the nuts.

"Maybe Andi sent them because you've been working so hard," Blake said, but he didn't seem to believe it himself.

"Are you sure you didn't send them so you could throw one at my brother?" I asked, giving him the side eye.

He grinned. "No, but I wish I had. Can I do that anyway?" He reached for a cupcake.

I swiveled around so they were out of his reach. "No, you can't throw a cupcake at my brother. If anyone is throwing a cupcake at him, it's going to be me."

"Sounds like a waste of cupcakes to me," Valentina said.

"I agree." I held out the box to offer her one. After all, I couldn't eat six cupcakes by myself. Okay, I could, but it felt nicer to share.

She hesitated before nodding her thanks and picking one up. Carefully, she bit into it. "Mmm, that's a good cupcake. Eastwood, get back to training." She waved him away with her spare hand.

"Yes, Coach," he said without hesitation. He gave me a smile before pulling his mask down and skating back to the goal.

I took a cupcake for myself before putting the box on an empty seat behind me. Even more carefully than Valentina had, I bit into it.

She was right, it was good. Whoever sent them must have ordered them from Doughballs. It was the only bakery in the city that made anything this delicious.

"Let me get this straight, someone sent you cupcakes and you have no idea who it was," Valentina said. She seemed genuinely curious, not judging me in any way. Of course not; she spent enough time being judged that she wouldn't do it to a colleague, especially another woman. I might even call her a friend. She was smart and supportive of those around her. If anyone was down, she was the first to lift them up. If they were up, she'd want to lift them higher. The team was lucky to have her.

I hoped Flynn would come to realize that, sooner rather than later. He was team captain, it was his job to hold everyone together, not to divide them because of... Whatever was going on in his mind.

"No." I told her about the note as well. I half-expected her to laugh, because who got notes from secret admirers? The whole idea was ridiculous. Was that something people did these days, outside of stalking?

Wait, I should stop and think about that for a moment. What if the cupcakes were sent by a stalker? That would be the ultimate irony. I spend my whole life making myself small and avoiding being noticed, when the one person who notices me is a nutcase.

Okay, the second person to notice me, because Blake made it very clear he did.

When he'd kissed me I knew it wasn't a joke. He wanted me as much as I wanted him. Whatever this was growing between us, it was real. He didn't want to be with me because he might gain something out of it. He wanted to be with me because he liked me.

It was refreshing, if slightly terrifying. He could break my heart into a thousand pieces but maybe it was worth taking a chance just this once.

Maybe things wouldn't end the way I always expected things to end. Was it time I started to live a little bigger?

"How romantic." Valentina sighed and her gaze slid back in Flynn's direction. Like before, her expression turned cooler. Guarded this time, rather than ice cold.

"It would be if I knew who was doing these things," I said. If it wasn't Blake and it wasn't my brother, who the hell was it? I couldn't think of anyone else.

One thing was certain, I was going to keep my eyes peeled until I figured it out.

Chapter Sixteen

Blake

"Let me get this straight, someone is sending things to Alice and it's not you?" Nate grinned.

I admit it, if he was telling me this, I'd laugh my ass off too. Right now though, I didn't feel much like laughing. I didn't know if someone else was into her if they were trying to piss me off. Either way, it was working.

"Yep. So far they sent her a letter, a box of cupcakes and some flowers."

The flowers arrived before we flew out for the first game of the playoffs. Yellow and white roses. They came with a card, but only her name was written on it. No declaration of love. Nothing to say who sent them. The guy who delivered them didn't know either. I asked. Even tried to bribe him with tickets. Apparently that wasn't enough to jog his memory. As far as I could tell, he genuinely didn't know.

"Sounds like you've got some competition," Nate said. "What are you going to do about it?" After a beat he added, "Does Cam know? About you and her, I mean."

I slowed down to swerve around a couple of people walking along the shore of Lake Ontario. I always liked a jog out in nature to calm the nerves before a game. Nate often joined me. All of the guys had their ritual, this was mine. Find somewhere green, preferably with some water, and jog.

"No, Cam does not know," I said finally. "There's not much to say. Alice and I have only kissed once—"

"You kissed Alice?" He glanced over to me without breaking his stride. "Things are getting serious then?"

"I don't know," I admitted. "She said she wants to give this a try, but if someone else is making a play for her..."

"You're not going to let that stop you?" He frowned. "Who are you and what did you do with Blake Eastwood? Since when do you not fight for what you want? You're not trying to tell me you can't compete with someone who sends cupcakes?"

"Of course I can," I said. "But maybe that's what she needs. Someone who gives her cupcakes instead of headaches."

"When you put it that way..." he said. "Although, you could also send her cupcakes."

"I think you might be missing the point," I said. "Couldn't she do better than someone whose idea of fun is filling people's shoes with glitter? Or putting Vaseline on their visor so they couldn't see through it?"

Nate laughed. "That one was epic. The look on Cam's face was priceless. I thought he was going to throw his helmet at you."

"It's nice to know you find gratuitous violence aimed at me amusing." I glanced over at him.

"We play for the NHL. Gratuitous violence is our bread and butter. Especially yours. Trying to slap a puck at you at a hundred miles an hour doesn't sound passive to me."

"They're not aiming at me," I pointed out. "But I get your point."

"Some of them are aiming at you," he said. "Usually in retaliation for something you've done."

"Which brings me back to Alice," I said.

"You think she might prefer a quiet life with Cupcake Man?" Nate asked.

"Wouldn't you?" I asked.

"Don't make me say something nice about you," he said.

I gave him a 'give it to me' gesture with my hand. "Be honest."

He sighed dramatically. "Fine. She could do worse than you. You're kind of okay."

"Kind of okay," I echoed. "Thanks. I think. You're kind of okay too. I guess Oaklyn could do worse."

"Oaklyn is too discerning to do worse," he said.

"Are you trying to imply Alice isn't discerning?" I asked.

"Actually, I think she'd have to be very discerning to date any hockey player," he said. "She knows what we're like more than most. She's seen the good, the bad and the messy as fuck and she hasn't run away screaming yet."

"Yet," I said. Maybe she should be running away. Screaming or otherwise. The fact she wanted to give us a chance spoke volumes. She'd seen the jokester and she'd seen the real me and she seemed to like what she saw. The real Blake Eastwood behind the practical jokes and silliness. The guy who cares about people and things.

"You think she will?" he asked.

"I don't know, but I hope not," I said. "I just wish I knew who was sending those things. I have no idea what he's getting up to while I'm out of town."

"Is that what's really bothering you?" he asked. "That while we're here in Toronto, he'll make a move?"

"I wasn't until you suggested it," I said. "You think Coach would notice if I took the first flight home?"

"Before the first game of the playoffs?" Nate asked. "I think he'd have your hide made into a hockey net."

"I could be part of the game forever," I mused jokingly.

"You wouldn't last that long," he said. "People would be lining up to hit pucks into you."

"Thanks for the vote of confidence," I said sarcastically. We reached the end of the pedestrian area, turned and started jogging back the other way.

Toronto was pretty in spring, especially on a sunny afternoon. The air was cold, but people were out enjoying the lake and the sights. How many had come to see the game tonight? The arena would be packed and I couldn't wait.

Nate opened his mouth to say something, but he was interrupted by the loud honk of a goose.

We exchanged glances and looked back over our shoulders. Out of a nearby bush, a goose stalked, her neck stretched out, wings raised at us in anger.

I turned around and jogged backwards, my hands raised to either side. "We don't mean you any harm."

The goose honked again. She lowered her head and lunged at us.

"I think we pissed her off," Nate said.

"I think so too," I said. "Run!"

I turned back around and bolted as fast as I could, while the goose chased after us, honking and flapping.

A couple of tourists stopped to watch, and film, while the mother goose chased us down the concrete walkway, past trees and benches.

We swerved and headed back into the city, where the thicker crowds must have deterred the goose from going. Or maybe she decided we were far enough away from her young, they were safe from us. She finally stopped following and headed back to her nest, looking satisfied with herself. Her strut reminded me of most of my teammates.

We slowed to a stop and stood with our hands on our thighs, trying to catch our breath and laugh at the same time.

"How long until that goes viral?" Nate asked. He looked over to the tourists and waved.

Did they recognize us? I couldn't tell, but the footage of two tall, muscular guys being chased by a goose was probably hilarious. I wouldn't blame them for uploading it and sharing it with the world. At some point, someone would recognize us and laugh even harder. I was fine with that. If they were entertained, then there was no harm done.

I grinned. "At least no one can blame me for that. I'm known for being pro-goose." Even ones who chased me down the street in Canadian cities. Although, this was a first for me.

"Some would say you are a goose." Nate grinned. As if that might offend me in some way.

"That is very true, my friend," I said. "We should get back before they start thinking we got lost."

"Right." His expression sobered. Of course it did, this was the first time the Sea Dragons made the playoffs in years. We needed to win tonight.

"We've got this," I said. "We're going to kick ass and not take any prisoners."

"That's good, because I don't think the team would like it too much if we took prisoners back to Lowball Bay." He straightened up and led the way back toward the arena.

"And they call me goofy," I said.

"You are goofy," he said. He eyed The Audience sculpture on the side of the Rogers Centre as we made our way past. Consisting of several sports fans with various expressions from angry to literally thumbing their nose, it seemed to give him the creeps.

"Just an average day in the life of a sports fan," I said. This was a baseball stadium, but hockey fans were no different. They were passionate and invested. Tonight, they wouldn't be on our side. That was okay, we'd win anyway.

"They're following me with their eyes," Nate said.

"You'd prefer they followed you the way the goose did?" I teased. "They could jump down from there and chase us down the street."

"Do you want me to have nightmares?" He grimaced. "Because that's the way someone has nightmares."

I chuckled. If the tables were turned, he'd be laughing at me too.

We passed the line of people waiting to ascend the CN Tower. I stopped to look at it. And up. At least as tall as the Hardball Tower in Lowball Bay, I'd never managed to find time to go up inside it. Partly because they didn't give us much time in any city we played in, partly because I didn't have the patience to stand in line that long. I made a note to ask Coach if he could organize a team visit up to the top. The view from up there would be amazing.

"No," Nate said.

"No, what?" I asked without lowering my gaze.

"No, you're not climbing the outside of it and tying someone's underwear to the top." He nudged me with his shoulder.

"I wasn't thinking that," I said. I would have eventually, but I hadn't gotten there yet. In another minute or two, the thought would have popped into my brain. The guy knew me too well. I'd have to try to be more unpredictable from now on.

Funny, I thought I already was but apparently not.

He snorted. "Sure you won't. If it wasn't that, then it was something else you shouldn't do. Didn't you promise to behave in return for Alice's help with the Ballet Academy building?" Help he'd also agreed to give, along with the rest of the guys.

I looked over at him. "And I have been. Have you seen me pull any pranks lately?"

"Seen you, no," he said. "That doesn't mean it hasn't happened."

"It hasn't," I said.

"What happens after you save the building?" he asked. "Do we have to start checking our shoes before we put them on again? Or our skates? Alice is going to have to go back to cleaning up your messes, isn't she?"

I remembered the look on her face every time she had to deal with some problem I'd caused. Frustration. Irritation. Dislike. I didn't want to go back to that. I also didn't want to stop enjoying my life. I was going to have to find a balance somehow. And I was going to have to make sure that by the time we saved the building, she was in too deep with me to want to walk away.

"I'll figure something out," I said. We headed to the entrance to the hotel, a short distance from the arena. "We should have insisted on Cam and Flynn jogging with us today."

It took Nate a moment to realize what I was suggesting. When he did, he grinned.

"I'd pay money to see both of them being chased by a goose." His eyes lit up as he imagined what that would look like. "Or better yet, Zack."

"Me too," I agreed. "Me too." At some point I was going to have to tell Cam about my relationship with Alice.

A goose chasing me might be preferable.

Chapter Seventeen

Alice

"And then, the goose takes off after them." Vivian tipped her head back and laughed. She'd watched the video umpteen times already.

I shook my head, but I couldn't keep myself from smiling. Thankfully, no harm was done to either player, or the goose, and the video *was* hilarious.

Funny things happened to the left side of my chest the first few times I saw it. Not so much the video, as the expression on Blake's face. I doubted anyone in the history of the continent had more fun being chased by a goose than him. His grin was infectious. Of course he enjoyed himself. He lived every day as joyfully as he could. Even when he was on the ice, concentrating, he was still living his best life.

People could learn a lot from him.

It's me, I'm people.

"And they won the first game of the playoffs," I reminded her.

Which seemed to have been forgotten thanks to the viral video. Not by the team's dedicated fanbase, of course, but the Internet in general. People were loving seeing him and Nate run through the streets of Toronto chased by an angry mother goose. They weren't the only ones she went after, but they were the most famous. The video going viral was inevitable. I hadn't even tried to stop it. Although, by the time I discovered its existence, it had been viewed a million times already. That cat was well and truly out of the bag.

"I was watching it." Her eyes were still on her phone as the guys stopped running and the video ended. "They did amazing. This video is just funny, that's all." She turned off her phone and placed it down beside her coffee.

"Yeah, it is," I conceded. "It's lucky neither of them were hurt." If they were, we'd be having a different conversation right now. If we were having one at all. I'd probably be at work, in damage control mode. Instead, I'd managed to sneak away and meet Vivian for lunch. Honestly, we should do it more often. She loved eating in other restaurants. If only so she could critique them. Just between me and her, of course. She was too classy to go around badmouthing other chefs.

"You don't want to kiss Blake better?" she teased.

Of course I did, but I kept my expression neutral.

"I don't want the team's star goalie injured so he can't play," I said.

She gave me a flat stare.

"What?" I stabbed a fork into a leaf of lettuce.

"Don't pretend you don't care about him," she said. "I see the way you look when I play that video. Like you want to gobble him down whole."

"I do not," I protested.

She cocked her head.

"Fine, I do," I said finally. "I like him, okay? I'm probably as crazy as he is, but I care about him. He's sweet."

When her expression suggested she wasn't letting up, I added, "Okay, he's more than sweet. I've never met anyone like him. He's dedicated to the things he cares about. He's passionate." If anyone was going to chain himself to a penguin, it would be Blake Eastwood. I couldn't believe I was even having that thought, but here we were. He was as protective of animals, people and old buildings as he was the basket out there on the rink.

"And he's hot," she said.

"And he's hot," I agreed.

"And he likes you." She popped a fry into her mouth. "Don't forget that part."

"As if I could," I said.

I couldn't stop thinking about that kiss. And the expression on his face when he saw those cupcakes. He looked as though he wanted to use his bare hands to tear apart the person who sent them.

I couldn't deny it, his possessiveness was sexy. My pulse raced a little faster thinking about it. That he cared enough to be jealous, even though he had no one to be jealous of. That is to say, I still had no idea who sent me those things.

Was it possible to be jealous of a complete stranger? I guessed it was, because I'd seen exactly that in Blake's eyes. I wasn't sure if he'd throw punches or cupcakes, but something would be thrown.

"And yet?" Vivian prompted. "Something is still holding you back. Is it your secret admirer? Don't tell me you're waiting for a better offer?"

"No," I said quickly. "No, I just... It adds another layer of complication."

Was there a chance she was right? Could it be that in the back of my head I was hoping my secret admirer was someone more like me? Less carefree. Less of a risk taker than Blake?

No. I dismissed the idea. I was reluctant to admit it to myself, but the fact was, there was no one better than Blake. If anyone asked me that outright, I'd deny it, but it was true. He was one of a kind, and I liked him for it. After all, don't they say that opposites attract?

"And..." She picked up another fry from her plate and pointed it at me. "Fess up."

"I'm worried there is no secret admirer," I said slowly. "What if it's one of his teammates trying to mess with us? He's not supposed to be pranking anyone, but that doesn't mean they aren't doing it back."

I didn't like practical jokes. I certainly didn't want to be the brunt of any. So far, I managed to avoid them. I knew there might come a time when that wasn't the case, but I'd hate it if this was someone's idea of a laugh.

In the back of my mind, I still wondered if Blake was involved somehow. Maybe not directly, but on the sidelines of someone else's plan to screw with me.

That didn't explain his reaction to the cupcakes. He was genuinely pissed off. As blindsided by them as I was. Whoever sent them, it wasn't him.

Added to that, I believed him when he told me the dickfetti was meant for one of the cleaning staff. He wasn't trying to get to me. Not with pranks.

Besides, I'd seen his handwriting in his notebook. It was different from the writing on the note. Big and bold like the man himself. Not arrogant, but confident.

"If that's the case, which one of them would it be? Your brother?" Vivian bit the fry in half.

"It's not really his style," I said. "Especially if he thought Blake was interested in me. He'd confront him, not send me flowers."

"Who then?" she asked.

"I suppose it could be Nate," I said slowly. "Zack might want to screw with Blake, but I can't see him doing something like that. Flynn either. I doubt it would be any of the coaching staff. Although, Valentina has a sense of humor and she did enjoy those lemon cupcakes as much as I did."

"But you don't think it's her either," Vivian guessed.

"No, and I doubt it's Andi. Her assistant, Rafe, is a possibility, but I don't see it being him either. He does have access to the management level though." I wouldn't put it past him to deliver the note on someone else's behalf.

"What about the GM?" Vivian asked. "He's handsome and you work pretty closely together, don't you?"

"Justin Carmichael?" I shook my head. "He seems cozy with his personal assistant lately. They used to hate each other, but then they were away for a few days and something changed." I didn't know the full story, and I sure as hell wasn't going to ask.

Vivian seemed disappointed. "I'm officially out of guesses. You're not sending those things to yourself are you?"

I made a face at her. "No, I am not. Are you sending them to me?"

"Now you mention it..." She grinned. "No, it's not me either. We'll just have to wait and hope they out themselves at some point. Especially if that's getting in the way of you and Blake."

"For all I know, the flowers were the end of it," I said. I hoped so. On the other hand, I didn't want it to stop dead, without me ever knowing who sent those things. I'd spend the rest of my life wondering and driving myself crazy. Not to mention I suspected Blake wouldn't let it go. It was better not to think about the extreme things he might do to find out.

"Alice North?" One of the restaurant servers stopped beside the table.

"That's me," I said, glancing up.

"Your meal has been paid for, including a generous tip. I was asked to give you this." She handed me an envelope and a receipt before bustling away.

"We spoke too soon." Vivian grabbed the receipt and looked at it, her eyes bugging out. "Generous is the word."

"Let me see." I took it from her and did a double take. "Holy shit."

I shoved my chair back and hurried to catch up with the server. "Excuse me, who paid for my meal?"

"I don't know," she said. She started to pack up dishes from an empty table. "They paid by phone and had the envelope delivered. Tell them I said thank you. My car needed repairs. Now I can pay for them." She nodded and hurried away.

I stepped back over to the table and dropped down onto the chair. "She doesn't know anything." I scooped up the envelope, opened it and pulled out a folded over sheet of paper identical to the first note I'd found under my office door.

"Let me guess, it has letters cut out from a newspaper?" Vivian said.

"It's handwritten." I showed her. Like the other note, it was only signed 'your secret admirer.'

I read it out loud. "*I hope you enjoyed your lunch. You deserve to have some time to relax. I know how hard you work. You're as amazing as you are beautiful. I'll see you soon.*"

I looked around, but as far as I could tell, no one was watching us. They were all engaged in conversation with the people at their tables. Except a couple who hadn't looked up from their phones the entire time.

"This is getting creepy," I said. How had they known I was there? I'd like to think it was a lucky guess, but what were the chances?

"You can say that again," Vivian said. "Where exactly is the line between secret admirer and stalker?"

"Right between sending flowers and knowing I was here having lunch with you," I said.

I read the words again, slowly and carefully. I still didn't recognize the handwriting, but it seemed to have been written in a hurry. Like they were worried they'd miss an opportunity. That I might be gone from the restaurant before they could have it delivered.

"They might be outside," Vivian suggested.

I glanced toward the door. "It's only a block back to work."

"I don't think you should walk it by yourself," she said.

"I don't think he means any harm," I said uneasily.

Assuming it was a him. Or even a single person. It could be almost anyone doing this.

Now I started to run through a list of people I potentially upset. That was a short list. Shorter than the list of people who could be doing this as a joke.

The advantage of spending your life making yourself small was that you were less likely to piss people off. It was difficult to be irritated by someone if you didn't know they existed. Not to mention I was always professional in everything I did.

I represented the Sea Dragons. The fact was constantly in the back of my mind, along with the fact I'd like to set up my own PR firm some day. The more squeaky clean I was, the better. How else could people trust me with their reputations?

"Are you willing to take that chance?" she asked.

I considered for a moment before shaking my head. Reluctantly, I picked up my phone and scrolled through my contacts before pressing on one.

Chapter Eighteen

Blake

"WHAT THE FUCK?" CAM STARED AT HIS PHONE.

"What is it?" I leaned over and looked, since he was holding up in front of him. I caught a glimpse of a message from Alice, but not the content.

"I have to go." He shot up out of his chair. "My sister is in trouble."

"I'll come with you," I said without hesitation. If Alice needed help, there was no way I was sitting out.

"What seems to be the problem?" Coach Lampton asked.

Cam glanced around, clearly uneasy at the idea of sharing. He must have concluded he wasn't going to be let out of a team meeting without an explanation. Not to mention that as an employee of the Sea

Dragons, everyone would find out sooner or later. His shoulders slumped slightly.

"Someone seems to be stalking her," he said. "She asked if I could walk her back from lunch. It's only a block away."

"Stalking her?" I rose, ready to find whoever it was and hang them from the flagpole. I couldn't rule out that I'd hang them from their balls. "Where is she?" I started for the door.

"Don't take long," Coach called out behind us.

I didn't stop to glance back.

Cam trotted to catch up. "What the hell, Eastwood? She's my sister. She doesn't need both of us walking her back here."

"She might," I said. "Are you willing to take that risk?"

That seemed to throw him for a moment. "I guess not. I don't know why you give a shit. I know you've been working closely with her recently, but..."

I slid him a glance.

He stopped in the middle of the corridor. "What the fuck? You better not be saying what I think you're saying."

"I didn't say a word," I pointed out. "But you're not wrong." And I wasn't going to apologize for it either. "Alice and I like each other."

He narrowed his eyes at me. "Is that why you've been so quiet recently? I haven't had to pull ping-pong balls out of my socks for weeks."

I grinned. "That was a good one." My smile slowly faded. "I promised her I wouldn't prank anyone in return for her helping me to save the ballet academy building. You know that." I assumed Andi would have filled him in.

"No one thought you meant it." Cam seemed conflicted. We got along pretty well, but this was his sister we were talking about.

"Should we talk about this later?" I asked. "If someone is trying to fuck with her, I don't like the idea that she's out of my sight."

He screwed his eyes shut. "I don't like the idea you said that." Slowly, he opened his eyes. "I like you, bro. You're going to have to give me some time to wrap my head around this."

I patted his shoulder. "Take all the time you need, dude. I'm not going anywhere. Now, where did you say she was?" I'd pull out my phone and send her a message if he didn't fill me in.

He told me where and we continued on down the corridor. "When were you going to tell me?"

"When there was something to tell," I said. "Alice is...taking her time. It must run in the family."

"Yeah, it does," he said. "Her more than me. She's always been the cautious one. I don't know how many times I've had to encourage her to take a risk."

"Did she take one once and it went badly?" I asked.

He glanced over to me before pushing out the front doors of the arena. "You'll have to ask her that." He looked cagier than usual.

"What did you do?" I asked. I should have guessed he was behind whatever happened. Who was better at giving childhood trauma than a sibling?

"Like I said, you'll have to ask her," he said with a grunt. I knew that tone of voice. He wouldn't be pushed any further.

Normally, that wouldn't deter me, but I got the impression this was something I should hear from Alice, not from him. If she'd open up to me.

"The person who sent the note, cupcakes and flowers, they did something?" I asked.

My heart was thumping hard in my chest. If anything happened to Alice... Forget world domination, I'd find a way to mobilize all the ducks in Lowball Bay to peck out some eyes. I knew I should have tried to bring that goose back from Toronto. She would have come in handy. Of course, the city had its own geese. I could—

Cam stopped so suddenly I almost ran into him. "The person who sent the what?" He shook his head. "I knew about the cupcakes, but there was more? Why am I only hearing about this now?"

"Alice didn't tell you," I guessed.

"No. In what world would she tell you and not me?" His brow creased, blue eyes heavy with confusion and irritation.

"In the world where she didn't want to bother you," I suggested. "She and I have been spending a lot of time together. That's how I know about it. Otherwise, she probably wouldn't have said anything."

Cam swore under his breath. "She should have told me." He resumed walking, faster now.

It was my turn to hurry to catch up, weaving through traffic until we reached the door to the restaurant. Cam strode in first, me right behind him.

Alice sat at a table to the side of the room, with another woman. They both rose when they saw us approach.

"What's going on?" Cam demanded.

Alice told him what happened and showed him the note. He read it quickly before handing it to me.

I turned around carefully, eyeing both it and the envelope for some sign of who sent it. As I expected, there was no name, nothing to offer a clue.

"I didn't want to bother you, I'm sorry," she said softly.

"You could never be a bother." Ignoring my teammate, I put my arms around her and pulled her to me. "You did the right thing in letting us know."

"What Blake said," Cam said. "I'm not going to ignore my sister when she needs help. "You're moving in with me and Andi until we find whoever is doing this." He sounded ready to peck out a few eyeballs himself.

"No," Alice said. "I'm not going to cramp your style. I'll be fine, I just freaked out for a moment. I shouldn't have—" She shook her head slowly.

"You wouldn't be cramping my style," Cam said, not looking convinced he was right. "You could always move back in with Mom and Dad for a while."

"You could move in with me," I said. "There's plenty of room at my place and I know Joe would like you. He's the complete opposite of me."

In the corner of my eye, I saw the other woman open her mouth to say something, but then close it again. When I turned to face her, Alice said, "This is Vivian, my roommate."

I smiled and offered a fist bump, which Vivian

returned. "It's nice to meet you. You don't mind me stealing your roommate for a few days?"

"I should probably resent the suggestion I can't keep her safe," Vivian said with a hint of a smile. "But who am I to stand in the way of true love?"

Love? Was that where we were headed? I didn't know for sure, but I liked the sound of it.

"I don't think it's such a good idea," Cam started.

"You're a newlywed who's about to have a baby," I pointed out. "Besides, Alice might be uncomfortable living with the boss."

"I live with the boss," Cam said.

"Then it's getting crowded," I said. "Besides, this will give Alice and me a chance to talk about the council meeting and publicity for the academy. Otherwise, we might have to all be at your place doing that."

Cam grimaced. "It's up to Alice," he said finally.

"I really don't want to be a bother," she said. "I overreacted and... I'm sorry. We should all get back to the arena." She stepped away from me.

I reached out to wrap my fingers around her wrist. "You are not a bother. Not even a little bit. If you prefer, I can stay with you. I can sleep on the couch. Joe would appreciate the peace and quiet for a while. And Vivian wouldn't be alone." Leaving her by herself didn't sit well with me either.

No, this was the perfect solution.

"I'll give you our address," Vivian said. She took my phone when I handed it to her and tapped in the details.

"Do I get any choice in this?" Alice asked, looking like she was hoping the earth would open up and swallow her. Honestly, if there was a shrinking potion she could take right now that would make her smaller, she probably would. As long as I could pick her up and keep her safe in my pocket, then I might even let her drink it.

"No," I said. "Even Cam isn't arguing." I jerked my thumb towards him.

"I'd feel better if someone was looking out for you," he said reluctantly.

She sighed. "Fine. But I'm not going to stop doing all the normal things I do daily."

I offered her my hand. When she took it, I led her towards the door and out onto the street.

Cam grumbled something, but followed, both of us watchful for anyone who might be looking at Alice the wrong way.

I noticed he hadn't punched me, so I guess he more or less approved of me and his sister. The way she laced her fingers with mine, she wasn't objecting either.

In spite of why we were here, this felt right. Walking hand in hand with her through Lowball Bay, back to the arena. What could be more natural?

"Thank you for coming," she said so only I could hear.

"I wouldn't be anywhere else," I said. We could be in the middle of the final game of the playoffs and I'd still bolt off the rink and run to her. Just like Cam did once when Andi was in trouble.

We loved hockey, but our women came first. Always.

"I'll have to swing to my place and grab a few things," I said after a moment.

"You really don't have to stay with me," she said.

"Yes, I do," I said. "I want to." I didn't care if I had to sleep in the bath, I wasn't letting her out of my sight if I didn't have to. "Don't worry, we'll figure out who's sending you this stuff and deal with them."

"They left a generous tip," she said in a tiny voice.

I frowned at her. "That does *not* make up for scaring the shit out of you," I said. "Never make excuses for assholes. They like to think they're good guys, but in the end, they're still doing the wrong thing."

"What if he didn't mean to scare me?" she asked. "People don't always think things through." She gave me a pointed look.

"And she slaps the biscuit into the basket," I said with a mock wince. "It doesn't matter what he intended. The end result is the same. That's not okay in my book."

She was right, though. I'd done a lot of things without considering the consequences. Including paying for people's meals without asking if I could. I doubted anyone minded and I'd never done it without them understanding it was me.

No, whoever did this didn't stop and think. Were they watching us now? If they were, I hoped they got the message.

Alice was mine. End of story.

Chapter Nineteen

Alice

"Are you sure about this?" Cam watched Blake wheel his suitcase through the door of my apartment, his eyes troubled. Clearly, he was skeptical whether or not this was a good idea. "You can change your mind and stay with Andi and me."

"Yes, I'm sure," I said. More so because of his skepticism. The whole overprotective brother thing was starting to chafe. Honestly, the whole situation was starting to chafe.

Regardless of their insistence, I should have walked back to the arena by myself. I didn't need them fussing over me. I certainly didn't need the looks I got when I returned to work. Mostly of concern, but how did everyone know so fast? Of course, guys were bigger gossips than women.

Andi even stopped by my office to check up on me. It was sweet, but not necessary. A stranger paid for my lunch, so what? For all I knew, he did it for lots of people. Generosity was nothing new.

I reminded myself the accompanying note was for me, no one else, and stepped over to the kitchen to turn on the coffee maker.

"Sorry I took so long," Blake said, rolling his suitcase over to a corner. "I figured I'd throw a few extra things into my case."

"I'm surprised you didn't bring three of them," Cam said. "Cases, I mean."

Blake grinned. "The other two are in my car." When Cam gave him a flat stare, he patted my brother on the shoulder. "Just kidding. If I need anything else, I'll go home and get it."

"As long as you remember this isn't your home," Cam told him, returning the pat with interest.

Blake ducked away from him. "Hey, careful with the moneymaker. We still have playoff games to win."

"I haven't forgotten," Cam said, without a hint of remorse.

"You should be focusing on that," I said. "Not worrying about me."

"We can do both," Blake said. "Sorry, I shouldn't

speak for Cam. *I* can do both." He stepped around the island, putting distance between himself and my brother.

Cam flipped him off. "I can worry about my sister, my wife and the playoffs all at the same time."

"Yes, but can you do all of that and this at the same time?" Blake picked up three apples from the fruit bowl and started to juggle.

I shouldn't have been surprised juggling was part of his skill set. He had to have exceptional hand-eye coordination to be a goalie in the first place.

"Did you learn that in clown school?" Cam asked dryly.

Blake laughed and caught all three apples before putting them back in the bowl with a flourish. "No, it was just a life skill I picked up along the way."

"Since when is juggling a life skill?" Cam asked. His skepticism was back.

"Since it was invented, about four thousand years ago," Blake said. "Who are we to question an ancient art?"

Cam slid me a look as if to ask if I was certain I wanted this crazy guy to stay here.

"Blake has a point," I said.

Blake opened his mouth.

Cam pointed a finger gun at him. "Don't say

anything about what points you have around me and my sister. I don't want to know."

Blake's lips curved upward. "I was going to point out how smart Alice is, but it's interesting your mind went there. I like you too, but your sister is cuter."

Cam made a face. "I need to get home. Take care of Alice. I don't need to remind you what would happen if anything happened to her."

"I know it involves an entire roll of tape, a packet of M&Ms and a turtle," Blake said.

Cam looked like he was about to ask, but shook his head. "Never mind, I don't want to know." He raised his hands to either side and stepped back towards the door. "I'll see you both tomorrow at work."

"Don't forget tomorrow's planned publicity event at the academy," I said. The team didn't want us standing outside with signs, singing protest songs, so I came up with a different angle. One Blake was looking forward to.

Cam groaned. "I forgot about that."

Blake grinned. "You're going to have the best time."

"Yeah, we'll see." Cam opened the door and slipped out before closing it behind him.

"What are those things for?" I asked. "The tape, the candy and the turtle."

"I have no idea," Blake admitted. "I could come up with something if you like?"

"Not if it's a real turtle," I said. "I have a sneaking suspicion it would be animal cruelty."

"Probably," he said. "Which I'm not into. But a plush turtle..." He seemed to be thinking things over in his head.

"I'm impressed at your ability to multi-task, but I think you should let it go," I said. "Cam is right, you should be focusing on playoffs, not ways to use an entire roll of tape."

He sighed. "Okay, I'll make a note to think about that later."

"I could give you a tour of the apartment," I said. "It won't take long. This place is pretty small." I'd seen the inside of several of the player's homes. My apartment was the size of one of their wardrobes.

"I'd love a guided tour," Blake said. "This place is cute." His gaze lingered on me, as if he thought I was cuter.

My face heated slightly. "This is the kitchen, obviously."

Great job, Alice, I told myself. *Your middle name should be Obvious.* Alice Obvious North.

Blake didn't seem as though he was judging me. He looked around the space with interest. "It's nice. I'm not much of a cook, but it looks functional."

"Vivian is a chef and she says it is," I said. I was far from an expert on the topic myself.

"That's her room." I pointed to a closed door to the side of the living room. "The bathroom is through there. We all share. My room is through there, and this is our beautiful view of the back of another building."

His place probably had a view of the ocean.

"When I first moved out of home, I lived in a place that had a view straight into a couple's bedroom," Blake said. "They used to get up close and personal with the lights on and the blinds open. Your view isn't so bad."

"Some people would enjoy that," I pointed out.

"Not when the guy is Gerald, from the accounts department." Blake stuck out his tongue like he just bit into something nasty.

"Oh." Gerald was a nice guy, but I didn't want to think about him that way. I'd never look at him the same way now.

"So, your room." Blake peered in the open door.

I suddenly felt like he was scrutinizing my childhood bedroom, looking for posters of pop stars and movie stars. Appraising the array of plush animals I had covering my shelves and bed.

Of course, I had none of that now. Just a bed, a couple of side tables and a wardrobe pushed up against the corner. It was nothing special, but I didn't do anything in there except sleep. Except the other night when I was thinking of him and my hand slipped down between my legs, my fingers rubbing my clit until I silently came.

Of course, he had no way of knowing about that, but I wondered if he guessed.

"You like blue," he said.

"It's my favorite color." All the covers and cases on my bed were aqua, with yellow accents. "Did you think everything I had would be pink?"

He glanced back at me and gave me a smile that made my heart thump. "I was guessing pale green. Something understated. I like the bright colors." He seemed surprised to see them.

"I suppose part of me is a rebel," I said. "But only in secret."

Of course he'd guess I had a preference for understated decor. It matched my personality. When I was a kid, I used to wear bright, clashing colors. Orange with green and purple. Now, I kept it for my bedroom.

"The couch is over there." As if he could miss seeing it.

"It looks comfortable." He stepped over and lay down, stretching out his full length.

I'd thought his feet might hang over the end, but the couch was a perfect fit.

Why was I disappointed by that? Okay, I could figure that out on my own. Some part of me hoped to have an excuse to let him sleep beside me. I wasn't going to let him sleep in discomfort. He looked like he belonged right there.

"I'll get you a pillow and some blankets." I kept spares in the top of my wardrobe, so I grabbed them and carried them back out to the living room.

"You have a *Teenage Mutant Ninja Turtles* blanket?" Blake took it and shook it out over his legs.

"It used to be Cam's." I handed him the pillow. "He was a huge fan when he was a kid." When he left home, I more or less adopted the blanket even if I didn't use it myself.

"What were you a fan of?" Blake tucked the pillow under his head and adjusted it before glancing over at me. "Let me guess. Wonder Woman."

"I was into Monster High," I said. "I liked how they were unapologetically themselves."

Blake grabbed my wrist and pulled me to sit

down beside him. "You don't feel like you can be unapologetically yourself?"

I averted my gaze. "Not really. Maybe if I had green skin and snakes for hair."

"I'm glad you don't, or you would have turned me to stone," he said. "Although, one part of me is turning to stone right now."

"Blake..."

"I care about you, Alice," he whispered. "A lot." He ran the pad of his thumb up and down the pulse point in my wrist, making my heart skip. "I'm falling for you. I know you feel the same way."

Before I could say anything else, he tugged me down to lie beside him and threw the blanket over both of us. He cupped my face with his hands and slanted his mouth over mine.

His lips were soft but insistent, his tongue pressing against mine until I parted them and let him inside. My hand on his bicep, I kissed him back. My blood thundered through my body, driving away all coherent thought. All that was left was to feel. To be in the moment for a change, instead of letting myself think too much.

He slipped one hand down to my shoulder, down my arm and across my belly. He left it there for a minute or two before moving it farther, down over the apex of my thighs.

I quivered at the touch of his fingers over the fabric of my jeans. I wanted more. So much more.

I whispered exactly that. "Please."

He eased open the button of my jeans and drew down the zipper before slipping his hand inside. He slid his warm fingers over my stomach and under my panties.

"You're so wet," he whispered. "Did I do this to you?"

"Yes," I whispered back. "Yes, you did." And then he was tracing circles over my clit with the tips of his fingers, stroking and rubbing until I shattered against his hand, my breath coming in pants and little moans.

"Fuck, Alice," he said softly. "You're so fucking gorgeous." He kissed my forehead before pulling his hand out of my jeans and doing the button back up.

"Blake..." Should I ask him to join me in my bedroom? "Would—"

The door rattled and opened. Vivian stepped inside. She saw us on the couch and her mouth formed an O.

"It looks like I'm interrupting something." She seemed amused rather than apologetic. Potentially glad she hadn't arrived home to see Blake bending me over the couch and pounding into me, but enjoying the fact we were getting closer. Emotionally, I mean.

Great, my thoughts were a jumble now. If that was what one orgasm did to me, then I couldn't wait to see what sex would do.

"No," I said quickly. "Nothing at all." Thank goodness she hadn't arrived a couple of minutes earlier. I scooted out from under the blanket and straightened it back up. "I should let Blake get some sleep. Um, good night."

Before either of them could speak, I fled into my bedroom and closed the door behind me.

Chapter Twenty

Blake

"This is bullshit," Zack snapped. "You can't be fucking serious?"

"I'm usually not," I said, pushing past him and heading up the steps into the ballet academy.

"I'm not doing fucking ballet," he snarled.

"No one is making you do it," Nate started.

"I am," Coach said. "You guys could do with some team bonding between games. Yeah, you won the first game of the playoffs, but you could have been more cohesive."

"I second that." Valentina followed him into the studio. "Especially in the first quarter."

"It was Blake and Nate," Zack said. "They were still recovering from being chased by that goose." He gave us a look like that was our fault.

"Zack is jealous we didn't take him with us," I said to Nate. I grinned at Zack. "Next time, we'll invite you."

Zack glared at me. "Will someone explain the point of this? We usually bond over dinner and a few beers. Not prancing around."

"It was my idea," Alice said.

He gave her an 'of course it was' glance, which she didn't wilt under. She was always steel under the small, soft veneer, but she was owning it today. I couldn't be more proud of her.

"Since we can't march up and down the street singing 'We Shall Not Be Moved', this was another way to draw attention to the importance of the building," Alice continued.

"Can we do that without making idiots of ourselves?" Zack asked.

"I'll be sure to cut anything potentially embarrassing before anything is posted to social media," she assured him. "It's not my intention to make any of you look bad."

He clearly didn't believe her, but he dropped his duffel bag to the side of the room along with everyone else's.

I stepped up beside Alice and whispered in her ear. "Don't worry about him. He has issues he needs to work through." I couldn't help breathing in the scent of her. Lavender and something that smelled like lemon. It better not be lemon cupcakes sent from any secret admirers. The smell made me hard and that was all kinds of conflicting.

I struggled to fall asleep last night after hearing her come. I needed a shower and took care of myself, while picturing her on her knees with her mouth around my cock. Getting off to thoughts of her was nothing new, but having her so close, just on the other side of the wall? That was something else.

I thought about knocking on her door and asking to join her but the way she'd run off, I figured she needed some time. So rub off it was.

"Don't we all?" she asked dryly. "I'm not worried about him. Just...everything else. The playoffs, the council meeting, the...you know. Secret admirer." She said the last in a whisper, not wanting the rest of the guys to overhear. They knew, but they didn't need a reminder. Not from her.

"It's a lot," I agreed. "But we've got this. This training session will draw attention to the building. Like Coach said, it'll help us bond." As for the secret admirer, I was keeping my eyes out. We all were. Alice was like a sister to everyone else on the team. If he tried anything with her, he'd answer to all of us.

"How lovely to see all of you here today," Linda said as she stepped into the studio. She looked around at us and beamed. "Don't worry, I don't expect you to be dancing Swan Lake. That's at least a lesson or two down the road."

"We're going to have more lessons?" Zack looked dismayed.

"Didn't you know?" I asked. "Coach signed us up for a whole semester of classes." I grinned while I said it.

"Fuck that," Zack grumbled.

"It's just one," Alice said. "You might surprise yourself by enjoying it."

"Exactly," I agreed.

Stranger things had happened, right?

Zack looked as though he'd prefer to pull out every hair from his chest with a pair of tweezers, but that seemed to be his default setting a lot of the time. I didn't know what it was, but like I told Alice, he had some issues to work through. Something was definitely going on at home, and I knew he wouldn't open up to me. Hopefully he was getting the help he needed.

"Let's start by stretching," Linda said, waving us all to the middle of the room.

Alice stood back, phone in hand, and filmed. A

film crew from the evening news stood beside her and did the same, along with one a couple of local newspapers.

If anyone did anything too embarrassing, she'd have to make sure they didn't share it with the world. Which they wouldn't, because access to the team relied on their goodwill. This was a good story without it turning into a circus.

"I was hoping they'd wear tutus," Valentina said from where she stood on the other side of Alice.

I grinned and called out, "I thought about suggesting it, but I figured the guys would politely decline." And by that I meant they'd say, 'fuck, no way.' Except me. I'd happily wear one.

"That and I want people to take this seriously," Alice said.

She was right. Most people don't realize how athletic dancing was. They would after this. The stretching, that would be easy, but we were going to work up a sweat.

"All right, let's start with some basic footwork," Linda said. "Let's start with the positions for your feet. This is first..."

The other guys looked from her to their feet, trying to copy the way she and I stood. To my surprise, Zack, who still looked irritated, seemed to know what she was referring to before she demonstrated.

Flynn, on the other hand, was struggling more than the rest of us. He wasn't complaining, he never did, he just didn't seem to know where to place his feet.

I returned my attention back to Linda, watching her fluid movements as she went through the footwork with practiced ease. Even having seen her do it a million times before, I was impressed.

Ballet helped with my flexibility, agility and concentration on the ice the way nothing else would, but I'd never be as graceful as her.

"I should have made them do this sooner," Coach muttered. He stood beside Valentina, watching us carefully. "We can add it to their regular training."

"Are you going to do it with them?" Valentina asked, teasing gently.

He snorted. "Nope, but I can watch. Make sure their heads are in it." He spent years playing for the NHL, but those days were behind him now. He still kept himself fit, but not at our level. He didn't have to, yelling at us was a workout in itself. Not to mention he spent as much time on the ice as we did during training.

"Shame, I would have liked to see you in a tutu too," Valentina smiled.

"Only if it's photoshopped," he said. After a beat he added, "Or dug up from my college days."

"Don't think I won't go looking," she said.

"Yeah, yeah, just don't go showing it to everyone," he said.

"I won't mention it to anyone outside this room," she said.

Considering there were twenty-five hockey players and a bunch of observers, and we were all listening, that photo would resurface in no time.

"I shouldn't have mentioned it," he grumbled. But he seemed to be holding back a smile. He wouldn't have brought it up if it bothered him that much.

I returned my attention to Linda, who instructed us to line up behind each other at the barre, one hand on the slim piece of wood while we slowly bent our knees.

Even Cam, who was directly in front of me, seemed to be...maybe not enjoying himself, but appreciating the workout he was getting. Shame Andi wasn't here, she'd get a kick out of watching him do this.

I looked over my shoulder at Nate, whose brow was creased as he tried to squat as precisely as Linda.

Flynn was directly behind him. He had no problem gripping the barre and doing squats, but he didn't seem to know what to do with his other hand. He held it out to the side as if he was balanced precariously.

Knowing him, he'd come back later for extra classes. He was the kind of team captain who was well aware of his behavior and the impact on his teammates. He'd do it to be a role model for us, to remind us there was always room for improvement. And he'd do it all without bitching. Which was more than I could say for a couple of the younger players, talking amongst themselves at the back of the barre.

I shot them a look until they settled down and paid attention.

"Okay, step back to the center of the room," Linda directed.

I lowered my hand from the barre and grabbed the hem of my shirt. I pulled it up to wipe sweat off my face.

I caught Alice staring at the grooves of my abs and the way the overhead lights made the sweat shine on the flat plains of my stomach. The V of my hips disappeared into my track pants. Her eyes follow the line down to my groin. Which was now feeling tight and heavy, like the night before, after I made her come on the couch. I was almost certain if Vivian hadn't come home when she did, Alice would have asked me to take her to bed.

Let's not have a boner in front of the whole team, I told my cock. Not to mention that I didn't need that to be tomorrow's headline.

I could see it now. *Sea Dragons' goalie gets turned on by dancing class.* Yeah, that would suck. The thought deflated me somewhat. Just enough to regain control and not be obvious.

"You should definitely post that on social media," Valentina remarked.

For a moment, I was worried she was referring to my erection. Shit. I was almost sure I got him under control in time. If I didn't...

Oh, Valentina was looking toward Alice. Good. Phew.

Alice glanced back at the coach. "What? Oh." Her phone was still on me, recording me wiping my face. Filming my sweaty but toned abs. Had Alice been ogling me with her phone? I won't lie, I liked it. She could film me anytime.

In case you hadn't noticed, I'm not shy.

I couldn't help being a little disappointed by the way she immediately turned the phone towards the other players. "I'll cut it out later."

"I don't mind if you leave it in," I said. I smiled as I dropped my shirt back into place.

"Leave it, the fans will love it," Valentina said. "A real life book boyfriend, hockey player. They love that kind of thing, don't they?" She gave a subtle flick of her eyes in Flynn's direction before her lips thinned.

"Yeah, they do," Alice said. Was that irritation in her eyes? It didn't seem to be directed at me or Valentina.

Was it the idea that other women would look at my body the same way she had? That they might see it and fantasize about me giving them an orgasm on the couch? That was both adorable and telling.

First of all, she was the only woman I wanted to give orgasms to. Second, and most important, she cared for me more than she realized. She might cut that footage out of the video she shared on social media, but I suspected she'd keep it for herself. That was fine by me, but I wanted her to see the real thing whenever she wanted to, not just a video.

We had plenty of time for her to see and touch. And for me to hear her come again and again. The rest of our lives if I had my way.

Chapter Twenty-One

Alice

"It looks like the video is doing what you hoped it would."

I looked up to see Blake leaning against the door frame. His arms were crossed over his chest, legs crossed at his ankles. When he wasn't looking for trouble, he was too attractive for his own good, especially like this. He wore a dark suit, crisp white shirt and a tie in the team colors. His beard was neatly trimmed.

The whole effect made me press my legs together. He was practically edible.

"It's generated a lot of interest in the academy building," I said. "And the publicity has been good for the team. Sponsors have been coming out of the woodwork to speak to Andi."

And the footage of Blake wiping his face with his shirt seemed to be shown on repeat all over the Internet.

He lowered his arms, stepped inside and sat on the edge of my desk. When it started to tip under his weight, he jumped up again, letting out a shout of surprise.

I had to grab onto my laptop to stop it from sliding off, holding it there until the desk stabilized again.

"Sorry, I thought that was more solid than it is," he said. He placed his fingertips on the side of the desk and wobbled it back and forth a couple of times. "Is this where you yell at me for sitting on it?"

"Why would I yell at you?" I moved my laptop back into place and lowered my hands to my lap. "Just because there's two perfectly good chairs on the other side of the room." I nodded over to them.

He grimaced playfully. "Chairs are for normal people. In case you hadn't noticed, I don't fit that description."

I snorted softly. "I might have become aware of the fact, yes." I was starting to like it more and more.

"What gave it away?" He pulled a chair over, turned it around and straddled it.

"The first time, I think it was the toilet paper

wrapped all the way around Cam's stick and fastened in place with rainbow tape." The expression on my brother's face was priceless.

Blake grinned, making my heart flip. "That was a good one. I'll have to do that again sometime. After the playoffs are over," he added quickly.

"I don't think you came here to talk about my brother," I said.

"I'm not saying he's not a fascinating subject of conversation," he said slowly, "but I came to tell you the council scheduled a meeting to talk about the building. It's on Wednesday at around two o'clock in the afternoon. You'll be there, won't you?"

"I'll certainly try," I said. I was invested in this now and I wanted to see it all the way through. The building and him. I hadn't gone this far only to walk away.

"Someone needs to keep an eye on me," he said without his smile faltering. "You never know what I might do otherwise."

I leaned forward and placed my elbows on the top of the desk. "You won't do anything to jeopardize the building. This is too important to you and to the city."

He cocked his head. "You're right, I won't. I'd never forgive myself if I screwed this up." He wasn't just talking about the building either. He told me the other night he was falling for me, and we hadn't had a minute alone since.

"I believe you," I said. After a moment I added, "You're an Internet sensation today."

He shrugged one shoulder. "Tomorrow, it'll be someone else."

"Not if you win tonight," I said. I stood and grabbed my laptop bag, sliding the device in before zipping it shut. "They'll be talking about you even more."

"Does that bother you?" He stood too.

"It's literally my job to make sure people are talking about you," I reminded him. "If they aren't, I'm not doing it right." In heels, I was almost as tall as he was. He could have leaned forward and kissed me, but he didn't.

Instead, he said, "You would never do it wrong." His tone was lowered, gaze dipping to my breasts.

My nipples tightened. "We should get downstairs. We'd both get in trouble if the star goalie missed his flight."

He looked like he wanted to argue, but sighed. "You're right, but if that desk was more stable, I'd take the chance." He grabbed my laptop bag and pulled the strap over his shoulder before gripping the handle of the suitcase I had stashed in the corner of my office.

If my desk was more stable, I might let him. Then we'd both be late, and there wasn't a person in the organization who wouldn't know why. That would definitely not be subtle.

"I can carry my own stuff," I said.

"Of course you can," he said. He didn't relinquish any of it as we stepped out of my office and headed to the elevators. The wheels of my suitcase rattled on the linoleum floor, sounding as uneven as they were. At some point, I'd have to consider getting a new one, but it would do for now. Until the wheels literally fell off.

"You like looking after people," I said.

I knew that about him, but it also meant arguing with him about carrying my things was pointless. He'd insist on doing it anyway. Honestly, it was nice to let someone do that for me for a change. Yes, I was an independent woman, but even independent women were allowed to accept help once in a while.

He flashed me a smile before pressing the down button. "Only people I care about."

"That seems to be everyone you've ever met," I said. "Including Zack Reed."

Yes, they clashed, but Blake wasn't the kind of

guy who'd turn his back on someone, even if they were being an asshole. If anyone could bring the left-winger around to become friends with him, it was Blake. How could anyone resist his warmth and sense of humor? I was certainly finding doing so increasingly difficult. Although at this point, I wasn't really trying. I was taking each day as it came.

"Don't tell him that, it'll go to his head," he warned. He wasn't denying it.

"I don't think he'd believe me anyway." I followed him into the elevator and let the doors slide shut behind us, leaving us there alone.

"Not in a million years," Blake agreed. He stood beside me, not quite touching, but close enough for me to be very aware of him. Warmth radiated off him like a hot wind from the desert. No, desert wasn't the right word. This was comfortable, with the potential to turn wet and sticky.

"If I haven't said it before, thank you," I said.

"You're welcome," he said before adding, "What for?"

"Looking out for me," I said. "Not judging me."

For seeing me when I was trying my best not to be seen. For not walking away even when I pushed.

"I'd never judge you," he said.

"Why not?" I turned to face him. "Haven't I

judged you?" I searched his gaze but found no condemnation there. No flash of insight that I was right and he should run away. Nothing to suggest he thought badly of me for making assumptions about him.

"You weren't judging," he said. "You were trying to figure me out. Which is totally fair, given I have more layers than an onion. Sometimes, I even smell like one." He wriggled his eyebrows.

I stared at him for a moment before laughing. "You do not smell like an onion."

Admittedly, the average hockey player didn't smell pleasant after an hour or two of sweating with all the padding on, but 'onion' was pretty harsh. Accurate when it came to some of the guys, but not Blake.

"You're right though, there's more to you than I first thought." So much more. So many layers to peel away, to reveal more.

"Okay, sometimes I smell like feet, but there's more to you too. You know what I think?" He adjusted the strap on his shoulder. "I think, deep down, you want a bit of the spotlight for yourself. Not a whole lot," he added quickly, "but a part. You don't want to be pushed aside and forgotten. I promise you, I'll never do either of those things to you." His expression was soft enough to melt the iciest heart, and he already thawed mine as it was.

"I—"

The elevator pinged and the door slid open.

Saved by the bell.

And the crowd of suit-clad players and team staff just outside the door. Equipment was piled to one side, ready to be carried onto the bus. The team's travel coordinator was moving through the throng, taking note of everyone and everything to make sure things ran as smoothly as possible.

"Eastwood!" Nate called out from near the door. "We were about to leave without you."

"You were not," Blake told him. "I'm too important to be left behind."

"You said 'Alice is too important to be left behind,' wrong," Cam said before offering Nate a fist bump. He eyed Blake and the way he was carrying my bag and pulling my bright blue suitcase behind him. For once, he didn't comment.

"Alice is definitely too important to be left behind," Blake said, ignoring their ribbing. "Who else is going to make us look good?"

"According to social media, you," Nate said. "Have you read the thirsty comments on that video?" He pulled out his phone and started to scroll. He stopped and read out loud. "*I just licked my phone.*" He read another. "*Can I call him daddy?*" And another. "*My ovaries exploded.* These women have it bad." He drew out the last word.

"Bad taste," Cam remarked, a smile twitching at the corners of his mouth.

These guys were like brothers, they meant no harm in anything they said to each other. Usually.

Blake flipped him off. "Have you heard the expression 'jealousy is a curse?' It's also not a good look for you two." He was as unruffled as ever, taking none of it to heart.

"No, it isn't," Flynn agreed, stepping up beside Cam. "The point of that class was team bonding, not to create friction."

"We are bonding," Nate protested. "We're bonding over a mutual appreciation of Blake. In fact, Cam was just saying he wants to start a new club, the Blake Eastwood Appreciation Society." He held his hands up in front of himself as though showing off a banner.

"I think it was you saying that," Cam said. "I said I'd join if you brought the beer."

"See?" Nate threw an arm over Cam's shoulder. "Bonding." He and Cam tilted their heads toward each other and gave matching, goofy grins.

Flynn hummed in the back of his throat. "Sure." He clearly wasn't buying a word of it, but he wasn't going to call them out either.

Blake shook his head and leaned over to whisper in my ear. "Will you join?"

My face heated and I didn't make eye contact with anyone as I whispered back, "I think I'm already a member."

He smiled, his breath brushing my lobe as he exhaled. "Great, I'll bring the cupcakes. And the condoms."

"You better uninvite my brother then," I said.

Before my panties were completely ruined, I took my bag and suitcase and headed over to where the other staff were starting to step onto one of the buses. I climbed up the steps and inside.

Chancing a quick glance back over my shoulder, I saw Blake adjusting his suit pants.

Chapter Twenty-Two

Blake

I KNELT ON THE ICE, MY ATTENTION GLUED TO the puck, and the players slapping it back and forth across the ice. Four times they got it past me.

Four.

I counted, but I didn't dwell on it. Now was not the time to contemplate failure or frustration. Not in overtime when the score was tied. Not when the Gulls were pressing our defense, trying to get in that one last shot.

In the corner of my awareness, the crowds were roaring. Screaming for their home team to take the win. Somewhere amongst all of that, Alice was filming the game. Her phone might be pointed at me right now. Taking in my focused expression as my eyes swiveled, ready.

The Gulls' winger tried to get past Nate, feinting to one side before skating to the other. Nate wasn't fooled, following him, stopping short of gaining possession of the puck.

The winger flicked the puck to his teammate, who took the chance. He skated by, trying to slip it past me. I saw the move coming and lunged to the side, stopping the puck before it slid into the goal.

The crowd groaned.

I grinned to myself and moved back, once again watching and waiting.

Flynn had the puck. He passed it to Zack, who flicked it to Cam right before one of the opposition players checked him into the boards.

Any other time, Zack would have shoved him back and maybe thrown a punch or two. Today, he shook it off and went on as though it hadn't happened. He wasn't going to let it stand between us and that one last goal.

Cam slid the puck back to Zack, who snapped his stick out like lightning, slapping the puck straight past the opposition goalie and into the basket.

The crowd went wild. Some booing, but most cheering a well-deserved win. Even if their home team hadn't won and was now out of the playoffs, we gave them one hell of a spectacle.

I stood up on my skates as the other guys flew towards me, flinging their arms around me and pushing me onto my ass.

Laughing, I managed to shove them off and get back up, my eyes scanning the crowds for Alice. She stood right behind the plexiglass, her phone not hiding her proud smile. I wanted to skate over, pick her up and throw her over my shoulder.

Since I probably smelled like onions or feet, I blew her a kiss instead.

She lowered the phone enough to give me a proper smile, just for me, before going back to recording the moment. How much of what she was filming now was usable? She was everywhere before, during and after a game, filming everything, but only a few minutes here and there ever reached the Internet.

I didn't know how she chose what to include and what not to, but it must be a lot more work than doing the filming. She seemed to enjoy it though, which was what mattered.

That and the fact we were still in the division playoffs. Two more wins and we'd take this thing. And from there, the Stanley Cup playoffs. Yeah, I was getting ahead of myself, but there was no harm in trying to manifest success.

I followed my teammates off the ice and into the visitors' locker room. Stripping down, I could confirm that I did indeed smell like feet. A problem that was remedied with a quick shower before I dressed in clean clothes and found a quiet corner to FaceTime my parents and Robbie.

"Blakey won!" Robbie said the moment the video call connected.

"Yeah, we did, buddy," I said, grinning to match his. "You were watching?"

"I always watch when you play," he declared. "Someone has to."

I laughed. "Yeah, they do. Thank you for being the one to watch. Were you cheering us on?"

"Nah! I was cheering for the Gulls." He cackled. "Just joking. I was cheering for the Sea Dragons. You almost didn't win." He shook a finger at me, but the tip and his fingernail was visible on the screen.

"But we did in the end," I said. "I had to keep you in suspense."

"Huh. Shut out next time, Blakey, okay?" He gave me his best stern expression.

"I'll try," I assured him. "Are Mom and Dad there? Can I talk to them for a moment or two?"

"Yeah." At the top of his voice he shouted, "Blake's on the phone!"

I winced, holding the device away from my ears.

"Someone in Vancouver, Canada didn't hear that," Nate said as he walked past.

I snorted softly, but otherwise ignored him. The phone crackled and the vision showed the carpet in my parent's house before their faces appeared, looking proud.

"Great game tonight," Dad said. "I thought they had you guys on the run for a while there." He glanced at my mother, who must have elbowed him.

"We wanted you to think that," I said. "We had that in the bag from the opening minute."

We hadn't, but that was my story and I was sticking to it.

"Of course you did," Mom said, although she obviously didn't believe it either. They knew enough about hockey to know we could just as easily have lost tonight. "I'm proud of you."

"It's good to know someone is," Cam teased as he followed Nate.

I flipped him off without taking my eyes off the screen. "Ignore him, he's just jealous his parents aren't as cool as mine."

"I don't think anyone would consider us cool," Dad said.

"Of course they would," I said. "You had me and I'm epic, so you must be pretty good too."

"I'm epic." Robbie stuck his head in front of Mom, grinning again.

"You sure are, buddy. I better go before they kick us out of the visitors' locker room." It was starting to empty anyway, of guys and equipment.

We had the rest of the night off, but an early flight home in the morning. Some of my teammates wouldn't even sleep until they were on the aircraft. They'd be busy having a couple of drinks and looking for someone to hook up with.

I just wanted to find Alice and somewhere quiet to be with her.

"What did you say?" I had to shout to be heard over the noise in the bar. Between the crowds and the music, I could hardly hear myself think.

"I said it's loud in here!" Alice shouted.

We'd more or less followed everyone down the street from the arena to this place. I'd wanted to do something else, but it wasn't every night we won a playoff game, so an hour or two of celebrating wouldn't hurt. Not to mention people wouldn't notice if we slipped away too early. Did I care? No. But Alice had Cam all but dragging her out to have a good time.

Tired of shouting, I grabbed her hand, pulled her off her stool and out of the bar.

The air outside was warm, with a hint of spring humidity typical to Florida. In a few weeks, it would be unbearable but tonight it was refreshing. Especially after the heat inside the bar.

"Is that better?" Lacing my fingers through hers, I led her across the road and over to a small park beside the water. Light reflected off the surface, glittering with each ripple of waves.

"Much better," she agreed. "I was starting to feel suffocated in there."

"Me too." I tucked her to my side and kept walking until we reached the edge of the water. "It's pretty here." I glanced over to her.

She was a hundred times prettier than the view, with her black jeans and red halter top that showed off her slender collarbones. The V of her neckline displayed a tantalizing amount of cleavage. Red heels completed the outfit.

"It is." She looked back at me as if she thought I was pretty. "I love Lowball Bay, but it's nice to get away and see other places."

"It is," I agreed, smiling because I accidentally repeated her words. During the season, we would have been back on a plane flying somewhere else by now. After a while, everywhere started to look the same. Airport, hotel room, rink, bus, airport. It all became a blur, broken up by periods of waiting for buses and planes and to check into hotels.

I wouldn't change a second of it, but being here with her made me wonder how many more years I could keep rushing around like I had been for the last few. At some point, I'd have to retire from playing hockey and figure out what I wanted to do with the rest of my life. All I saw right now was a future with this stunning woman beside me. Nothing else made any sense.

"Do you like pools?" I asked.

"You're not going to throw me in one are you?" She looked around us, but there wasn't one in sight.

I chuckled. "No. When I was a kid I used to go to my friends' houses and swim in their pools. I always thought rich people had them. It wasn't until years later I realized none of my friends were rich. Not like crazy rich, you know? But it stuck with me anyway. My apartment building has one, but I've always wanted a house that had one."

"You could buy one," she said.

I could buy several, to be honest, but that wasn't the entire point.

"I wanted to wait," I said, watching the rippling water. "Until I had someone to choose a place with. Otherwise I feel like I'd be moving them into my place. I always wanted it to be our place. Does that sound stupid?"

"Not at all," she said. "I think lots of people feel that way when they move in with someone. Like the space belongs to one or the other of them."

"Exactly," I said. "I feel like the apartment I live in is more Joe's space than mine. I'm just keeping my stuff there for a while. Don't get me wrong, he's good company; that's why I have a roomie."

It wasn't about saving money, it was because both of us traveled so much for our jobs, it was good to know someone was around when the other wasn't. Otherwise the place would be empty a lot of the time. Personally, I didn't want to come home to an empty apartment, or an empty house.

"So, you're waiting for the right person to come along to pick a house with?" she asked. "If I tell you I don't like swimming pools, does that mean the whole thing is off?"

I glanced over to see her arched eyebrow and the question in her eyes.

"No, I'd pivot," I said easily. "Just like I do out there on the ice. If you want something enough, you have to be prepared to be flexible." After a beat I added, "You don't like pools?"

"I've never really given them much thought," she admitted. "Now that I think about it, I don't mind them. But I prefer the ocean. I've always wanted to learn how to surf. And scuba dive."

"Is that why you like blue?" I asked. "Because it reminds you of the ocean?"

"Something like that," she agreed.

"So a house with a pool, overlooking the ocean," I concluded. "Walking distance to the beach. Or beach front."

"Don't," she whispered.

"Don't what?" I frowned. She didn't like this daydream?

"Don't paint a beautiful picture like that," she said. "If you do, I might find myself wanting it."

"It's okay to want things." I slipped my arm around her and pulled her closer.

"I don't want to want things and then never be able to have them," she said. "I'm a realist."

"So am I," I said softly. "There's no reason we can't have everything we want."

Before she could say anything else, a voice

shouted, "There he is! Blake! Blake! Can we have a selfie?"

Alice stepped aside as a group of women converged on us.

I smiled for a few selfies and gave a hug here and there before I registered Alice was gone. I looked around, but there was no sign of her. She slipped away while I was interacting with fans. Letting me have the spotlight again.

Or was the idea of forever what scared her away?

Chapter Twenty-Three

Alice

I RUBBED MY EYES. A GLANCE AT THE TIME ON the top of my screen told me I'd been poring over footage for the last three hours. I made, captioned, hashtagged and scheduled at least a dozen reels and twice as many photos. Enough content for the next week.

I opened the top drawer of my desk and pulled out a bottle of eye drops. Tilting my head back, I dripped two drops into each eye before squeezing them shut and letting it work.

Staring at the laptop for so long made my eyes dry, and at times painful. Hazard of the job. One I didn't mind. I genuinely enjoyed making content for social media. It was something I was good at. Trying to figure out what would resonate with fans and what wouldn't. It was like a big jigsaw puzzle.

I put the bottle back in the drawer, closed it and pressed play on the next section of footage. This was taken during a break, when the guys were on the side of the rink, catching their breath and quenching their thirst.

Blake pulled off his mask and helmet, leaned back against the boards and tipped water from his bottle all over his head. It poured down his hair and the sides of his face. He shook his head, sending droplets flying every which way, before standing upright and grinning in my direction. His teeth were white behind his beard, his eyes shining more than his wet hair. He squirted what was left in his water bottle into his mouth and swallowed, his Adam's apple bobbing.

Behind him, several women watched him avidly, eyes wide. Most with their phones in their hands. They weren't the ones who sought him out after the game, while we were sharing a quiet moment by the water. These women were older, but no less entranced by the sight.

So was I.

I didn't remember pressing pause, but I found myself staring at him on the screen. Him smiling back at me like I was the only person in the world. Like that smile was all for me.

For a moment, I'd let myself think that was how it was. But then those women rushing up to get his attention reminded me who he was. He was the goalie for the team I worked for. It was my job to raise his social media profile. I couldn't complain when that was what actually happened.

Not, I reminded myself, that it was all me. Blake was charming and charismatic. He'd started clowning around to draw attention from his brother, but he didn't need to. He could get people's attention by being himself. This was the curated version of his working life. A collection of carefully edited moments, like the rest of social media. Nothing on there was real, including this. But damn, it looked good. He looked good. I thought back to the conversation before we were interrupted.

"Don't paint a beautiful picture like that," I said. *"If you do, I might find myself wanting it."*

"It's okay to want things." He slipped his arm around me and pulled me closer.

"I don't want to want things and then never be able to have them," I said. *"I'm a realist."*

"So am I," he said softly. *"There's no reason we can't have everything we want."*

The words echoed around and around in my mind like a reel on replay. Could we really have all of those things? He seemed to believe we could. I hardly dared to let myself want them. What else did I want that I didn't let myself have? Too many things if I was honest.

For years I thought about starting my own PR company, but I never took the leap. Maybe it was time I took a step outside of my self-made box.

I shook my head to myself and reminded myself to focus on my job. Fans would want to see more inside footage of the last game. Waiting for me to upload it for their enjoyment.

I pressed play as Coach Lampton called for the guys to return to the ice for the fourth period. Valentina said something to him which the phone microphone didn't catch, but whatever it was made Lampton snort, and her grin. She gave the camera a finger wave before returning her attention to the ice.

I carefully separated both sections of footage into separate reels. Blake for the thirsty viewers and the two coaches for a different demographic of fans. Plenty of women liked to see Valentina as much as they wanted to see the players. She was a terrific role model for women and girls everywhere. It didn't hurt to remind people that hockey was about more than fistfights and thirst traps. It was also about people working hard to fulfill their dreams.

If one person was inspired by her, then we were both doing our jobs. Although, I wanted more than one to follow her example. A lot more.

I uploaded the first video and let it play a few times while I considered a caption. Okay, and enjoyed the view. If he looked this good while fully dressed and heavily padded, how would he look in the shower?

You can guess where my imagination went right then. Instead of naked and wet stepping out of the shower, he was climbing out of a swimming pool. A nice private one, with high fences on two sides and a view of the ocean on another.

He smiled at me before slowly walking towards me, his cock thick between his thighs. He reached for me, pulled me to him before lifting me up and wrapping my legs around his waist. He positioned himself before slowly sliding into me. Slowly, he started to move.

"Earth to Alice, come in, Alice." Fingers snapped in the side of my vision, making me blink and crash back down to reality.

"Cam." Of all the people catching me daydreaming about his teammate. My face was so hot it must have been bright red. There was no way he wouldn't notice.

"I'm sorry, I..." I looked up at him.

Stared.

Okay, maybe he wouldn't notice I was flushed. Right now he seemed to have other things on his mind.

"What the hell?"

His hair was wet and slick, and filled with sparkling pieces of glitter that shone in the overhead light. I'd seen dresses less sparkling than he was right now.

"What did you do?" I asked. And how did I not know glitter came in that shade of green? He looked like a walking Saint Patrick's Day parade. Usually I'd suggest it wasn't his color, but today it looked pretty perfect.

He poked a section with the tip of his finger. "As far as I can tell, it's egg white, mixed with a shit ton of glitter." He held up a finger which was now coated in lime green glitter.

I bit back a smile. "Of course it is. Why do you have egg and glitter in your hair?" I wish I could say it was the strangest thing I'd seen, but it wasn't. Not by a long way.

I struggled to keep myself from laughing my

head off. Cam was always so put together. Seeing him like this was hilarious.

"I was hoping you could answer that," he said. "I went to wash my hair after training and found my shampoo switched out with this." He jabbed a finger in the direction of his head.

"I didn't do it," I said. A tiny part of me wished I had.

"I'll give you one guess who did," he said.

"You think it was Blake?" I cocked my head at him. "He promised not to pull any pranks until after the playoffs."

"Who else would have done it?" Cam asked. "This is classic Blake."

I couldn't argue with that. This was exactly the kind of thing he pulled.

"Okay," I said evenly. "Have you asked him about it?"

Cam looked at me as though I asked him if he was sure that the sky was blue. "I can't find him. I figured he might be up here with you."

"I haven't seen him," I said. After our conversation in Florida, I went back to my hotel room and slept until we left for the airport. When we got home, I made excuses to stay in my room. We'd had team meetings and obligations since. A couple of times he looked like he was going to say something, but evidently he decided to give me some space instead.

That was what I assumed until now.

"When you do, tell him it's game on," Cam said. "If he wants to fuck around, he's going to find out." He didn't look annoyed. He looked like he'd been given a challenge and was trying to figure out how to respond to it in order to go one better. Men.

"It could have been someone else," I pointed out.

Cam shrugged. "More fun for me."

"Shouldn't you be focusing on your pregnant wife and the playoffs?" I asked.

Both of those things were more important than revenge, right?

"I can focus on more than two things at once," he said. "Or I could delegate the prank to you. You never know, you might enjoy yourself."

I gave him a flat stare. "Not after last time."

He smirked. "That was ten years ago, Alice. Does it really bother you? Still?"

I shifted uncomfortably in my seat. "You know what happened. It was my fault for listening to you and doing it in the first place."

"If you hadn't, I would have," he said.

"Then you'd be living with the consequences," I

told him. "I'm not helping you prank Blake, or anyone else. I'll talk to him. Please don't do anything stupid."

"When have I ever done anything stupid?" He grinned.

I picked up my phone. "Wait a minute, I think I have a list on here somewhere."

"Ha ha," he said sarcastically. "It would be the world's shortest list."

Since I didn't want to pick a fight with him, I decided not to remind him he almost committed himself to a woman who was only interested in him for who he was and what he could do for her modeling career.

However, I did take a photo of him with his hair full of glitter.

"Fans are going to love that." I grinned at him.

"You are not putting that online." He pointed at my phone.

"Why not?" I pretended to look innocent. "It's my job to put interesting content about the team on the Internet. What could be more interesting than Cam North covered in egg and glitter?"

"You suck," he told me. "I knew I should have washed it off before I came up here."

"Not your first mistake and it won't be your last," I said. "But I might hold the photo back if you agree not to retaliate." Yes, I wasn't beneath blackmailing someone. Especially my brother.

He scowled. "I can promise not to retaliate until the playoffs are over, but that depends on Blake. If he pulls anything else, all bets are off."

"I'll talk to him," I said.

As funny as it was to see Cam looking the way he was, if Blake did this to him, then he broke his promise to me. I didn't want to believe he'd do that, especially given what was at stake. Would he really throw all of that away just for this?

Yes, it was funny as hell, but a broken promise was a broken promise.

If he'd break that, then what else would he break?

Chapter Twenty-Four

Blake

CHAIRS SCRAPED ACROSS THE FLOOR AS PEOPLE moved to sit. Others gathered in groups to talk in low voices, like a hive of buzzing bees.

"This is something," Nate remarked. He leaned against the wall at the back of the room beside me. "I didn't know so many people were interested in saving old buildings."

He crossed his arms over his chest, his gaze scanning the room slowly. Before Oaklyn, he would have found someone to hit on by now. Now, he stayed back with me, observing.

"They usually aren't," I said.

The amount of people who gathered outside waving signs surprised me, as did the number who managed to get a spot inside the Council room.

Apparently we reached people the way we hoped we would. Go us.

I scanned the crowds, trying to find Alice, but only caught a glimpse of her dark ponytail beside Andi's cloud of red curls. Cam stood with them, tall enough to be seen over both of them. They shuffled over as someone stood to offer Andi their seat. Any other time, the independent woman would have declined, but today she looked grateful and lowered her heavily pregnant body down to the chair.

"It was me doing pirouettes, wasn't it?" Nate's voice drew me back to him.

"It was absolutely you doing pirouettes." I grinned. "You're an inspiration to people everywhere."

"Why do I feel like that was a backhanded compliment?" He crinkled his brow. "Because I could do them, anyone could?"

I wasn't trying to imply that, but if that was what he went with then I'd roll with it and grin.

"Just remember, you said it, not me." We hadn't done anything that technical, but now I wished we had. Seeing him trying to pirouette would have been one hell of a sight. On the other hand, he'd probably do better than Flynn. He'd most likely fall on his ass. Also something I wouldn't mind witnessing.

"You suck," Nate told me.

"That's not the first time anyone's told me that and it won't be the last." I shrugged. "Just the most recent."

"I bet Cam had a few things to say this morning." Nate gave me a sly look.

It was my turn to frown at him. "About what?" I'd done an extra training session with the goalie coach this morning, focusing on tightening up a few areas that needed work. No matter how good I was, there was always room for improvement. The other guys were finished and gone before I stepped into the locker room for a shower.

"Someone switched his shampoo for egg whites and glitter," Nate explained. "He looked like a tall leprechaun."

That was an oxymoron if I ever heard one.

I snapped my fingers. "And I missed it? You took a photo, right?" Cam covered in green glitter would have been funny as fuck. I could picture his expression now. He wouldn't have been laughing.

"He wouldn't let us," Nate said regretfully. "Are you trying to say you didn't do it?"

I frowned at him.

"Can we have some order please?" one of the

council members, a woman in her mid-sixties, called out.

Nate looked at me like the conversation wasn't over, but turned his attention to the front of the room with everyone else.

After a minute or two, the place fell quiet.

"Thank you everyone. Today we've called this meeting to discuss the proposal regarding the Lowball Bay Ballet Academy building on Eel Street. At this point I'll remind you anyone who becomes disruptive will be removed from the council chambers."

She gave us all a stern look, like a teacher with a rowdy class. Unlike school, becoming disruptive in a place like this could get a person arrested. The fact of which I was sure we were all well aware. I could afford the fine, but that kind of publicity would follow me for the rest of my career.

For something as important as this, getting rowdy was a last resort.

Nate cut me a look as if he thought I planned something to cause an uproar. I hadn't. Honestly, it hadn't crossed my mind, which surprised me as much as it would surprise anyone.

Although, it might set our cause back if I did something messy, so it was just as well I hadn't.

I shook my head at him and looked away. My gaze found Alice, who watched me with a similar expression on her face. Was that all everyone thought about me? That I'd jeopardize the building just for shits and giggles?

Okay, egg white and glitter was something I'd do, but I wouldn't fuck this up. It was too important. Apparently I had a filter after all. Who knew?

I gave Alice a smile. She gave me a tentative one in return and nodded before looking towards the council members who sat behind their tables. Cam must have noticed the direction she was looking, because he glanced over at me before raising his fingers to his eyes and then pointing them toward me.

It seemed like everyone was keeping an eye on me. They'd be shit out of luck if they thought I was up to something.

I stuck my tongue out at him before looking away as one of the city's property developers rose to give his pitch as to why the building should be torn down and replaced with a high end apartment building.

I have to admit, by the time he finished speaking, I almost liked his suggestion. If he built it anywhere else, I might even buy an apartment and live there.

"Thank you, Mr. Collins," the Councilwoman

said, gesturing for him to take a seat. "Now we'll hear from the opposing point of view. Linda Silva and Blake Eastwood."

A ripple of surprise went through the room. They hadn't expected me to step forward and speak. Except Alice. She and I worked on what Linda and I should say, reminding me to speak from the heart.

As if I could do otherwise.

I stepped through the crowd that parted for me, to the head of the room where Linda stood, looking anxious. She held her hands in front of her, wringing them slowly. She swallowed visibly, blinking faster than normal. Her hair was up in its usual bun, but her outfit was businesslike. Knee length skirt and black blouse with puffy sleeves.

"We've got this," I said softly. "These people are all behind us."

"Are they?" she whispered. "Those apartments did sound nice. The city needs..."

"We need to preserve our heritage," I said firmly. "That building is a piece of history."

I raised my voice so everyone in the hushed room could hear.

"It's easy to tear down places and replace them with steel and glass. Places that may have amazing views over the ocean, but do they have the memories this building does? Have thousands of feet walked those floors? Have thousands of aspiring dancers found their place in the world? How many people have danced there and gone on to careers in the arts? As dancers. As choreographers. As costume makers, lighting people, even composers? How many people have used the skills they learned there for other things like playing ice hockey? I know I have. You can't replace something like that."

I took a breath, aware every eye was on me.

"But there's more to that building than memories, because memories are, after all, portable. It's also one of the oldest buildings in the city. One of the most beautiful. Why would we want to tear that down and replace it with another building that looks the same as all the rest? In some ways, I have something in common with that building. In fact, we all do. We're all unique and individual. Special in our own way. I don't know how many times I've heard people say if we all liked the same things, how boring would the world be? Do we really want Lowball Bay to be boring? I know I don't." I pressed a hand to my chest.

"I want our city to be interesting and different. Diverse. I want people to come here and see things they can't see anywhere else. How many people have been on social media and seen photos of other people's holidays? Do they take photos of shiny new apartment buildings? Maybe, but a lot more take photos of historic places. Beautiful places. That's exactly what this building is. It's a landmark. It's iconic. And it deserves to remain standing."

I nodded and took a step back. For what seemed like a year, I thought my words fell completely flat. Okay, fine. I was a goalie, not a public speaker. But then the room erupted in cheers and clapping.

Linda wiped tears from her eyes. "I couldn't have said it better myself."

I placed a hand on her shoulder and squeezed before looking to where Alice crouched, filming us, her phone in front of her. None of what I said was what we'd rehearsed, but she seemed pleased. Maybe even proud. She smiled at me, lowered her phone and clapped one hand against her opposite wrist.

"Thank you very much," the Councilwoman said. "It seems we have a lot to consider. We'll discuss the matter at our next meeting and give our final deci-sion as soon as we reach one."

I scanned the gathered councillors, but couldn't determine which way they might vote. I could only hope what I said helped to sway them to vote our way.

"What do you think they'll do?" Linda asked as we started to file out of the room.

"I don't know." I caught the eye of the developer who wanted to tear down the building. I expected hostility, but instead I saw grudging respect. I nodded, giving him the same. His proposal was a good one, for somewhere else.

I turned from him to Alice, who stood near the doorway, waiting for me.

"I know that wasn't what we worked on—" I started.

She threw her arms around my neck and pulled me close. "That was perfect. There's no way that's not going viral."

I stiffened slightly. "I didn't say that for it to go viral."

She drew back, her eyes on mine. "I know you didn't, I just... It will. It's going to generate more publicity for the cause. Just like we planned."

"Right, of course," I gave her a squeeze before draping my arm over her shoulders and stepping out the door beside her. "That was the point."

Then why was I starting to feel like a performing monkey? I never minded the publicity before. What was different now? I suppose it was because social media stunts for the team were one thing. This was a lot more personal.

I couldn't argue that we needed people to know about this, so we could get their support, but I felt more exposed than usual. Like I was sharing a part of myself the world didn't know about. Because I was so used to hiding behind the clown façade, not showing that I had a softer side.

I wasn't used to feeling vulnerable.

"I need to ask you about something," she said.

I offered her a smile. "You can ask me about anything," I said.

For her, I was happy to be vulnerable. I could be myself around her in a way I couldn't around most people. Comfortable. Like we fit together, puck in catcher. Biscuit in basket. Okay, maybe that wasn't the best analogy for a goalie, whose job it was to keep the biscuit away from the basket, but close enough.

"Alice! Alice!" Cam was pushing through the crowds to get back to us. "I have to go. Andi's gone into labor."

Chapter Twenty-Five

Alice

"You don't have to stay if you don't want to."

I sat beside Blake in the hospital waiting area. We'd followed my brother and Andi before they were led into the delivery room. That was an hour ago now. Some babies, like my brother, took thirty hours or more to arrive, so it could be a long time yet.

"I want to." He curled his fingers around my hand. "I like being here."

"In hospital?" Like any player, he'd had his share of injuries and probably liked the place as much as I did. Which was to say, not very much.

"With you," he said, giving my hand a squeeze. "You really liked my speech?"

"I loved your speech," I said sincerely. "It was

better than anything we talked about." Better than anything I would have come up with, which didn't surprise me at all. I told him to speak from his heart and he had. People always did better when they were their best, authentic selves. There wasn't a person in that room not moved by his words and conviction. If things went our way, it'd be because of him.

"I just said what needed to be said." He shrugged modestly.

Speaking of what needed to be said.

"I saw Cam this morning," I started slowly.

Blake's brow creased with confusion before he started to smile. "I heard he had a disagreement with some glitter. I wish I was there to see it."

"I'm sure you do," I said. "He wasn't happy about it."

"He might have preferred blue," Blake said, his head cocked thoughtfully. "Or bright pink." He seemed to be mulling over the options, the sides of his mouth curved up.

"Did you do it?" I blurted out.

His smile faded. "What? No." He paused for a beat or two. "That must have been what Nate was getting at. He seemed to think I pulled something."

"But you didn't?" I tugged my phone out of my pocket and showed him the photo of Cam.

He tipped his head back and laughed. "That's fucking awesome, but it wasn't me. Whoever did it, I want to buy them a beer." He raised an eyebrow at me. "It wasn't you, was it?"

I turned off my phone. "No, it wasn't me. Have you got any idea who it was?"

"None. You really thought it was me, didn't you?" He lowered both eyebrows, knitted them. "I promised you I wouldn't pull any more pranks until after the playoffs."

"I know you did," I said slowly. "I just... I thought..."

"That I couldn't resist doing it anyway?" He sounded hurt. Blue eyes regarded me intently. "I look like a clown on the outside, but I never break my promises. Especially not to you. I care about you, Alice. A lot. I need you to know you can trust me."

I glanced down at the worn linoleum floor. "I know, I do..."

"It doesn't sound to me like you do," he said, his voice tight, like he was fighting himself for control. "Do you think I'd throw it away, throw us away, for some glitter? I promise you, I didn't. I wish I was there to see the look on your brother's face, but I wasn't. What sort of clown pulls a prank if they aren't there to see the result?"

I shrugged. "I don't know, it's not my area of expertise."

"What happened?" he asked softly. "Cam said you did something once but he wouldn't tell me what it was."

I exhaled softly out my nose before looking over at him.

"You'll think it's stupid."

"Have you met me?" he asked. "I'm not going to judge you, no matter what you say. Unless you eat pickles and ice cream."

I grimaced. "Together? Ewww, no. It's worse than that." I sucked in a breath through my nose and hoped he meant it when he said he wouldn't laugh at me. Anyone else, they probably would. I was about to find out if I really could trust him.

I started slowly.

"When I was about fifteen, Cam dared me to make a cake for a meeting my mother had to go to. She was always the one who took cupcakes and cookies to the office on a Friday, you know?"

He nodded and gestured for me to continue.

"The cake I made was hollow," I said. "Then

filled with sprinkles. When it was cut into, it collapsed, spilling sprinkles everywhere."

Blake grinned. "That's awesome."

I snorted softly. "It would have been awesome, but thousands of those sprinkles were spilled onto the lap of my mother's boss. The meeting she had, it turned out they were thinking of promoting her."

I screwed my eyes shut and shook my head. "Her boss was furious. She didn't get the promotion. In fact, she was fired. Because of me."

"Shit," Blake whispered. "Okay, I can understand why you don't like pranks."

"Yeah, that backfired hard," I said. "My mother should have been given a corner office, but instead she was kicked out. Because of me."

"Who was kicked out because of you?" Cam stepped out of the delivery room. Before we could ask, he held up his hands. "It'll be a few hours yet. I just ducked out to get some food."

"We can get it for you," I offered, rising to my feet.

He gave me a hug. "That'd be great, sis, thanks. But tell me who got kicked out of where first?"

"I was just telling Blake about the cake I made that got Mom fired," I said weakly.

He leaned back and looked at me, confused. "The cake that..." A slow smile crept onto his face. "She wasn't fired, Alice. Her boss admitted she'd already chosen someone else, before the cake incident. Mom got a better offer from the people she works for now and quit."

Now I was the one looking at him in confusion.

"She wasn't fired? Because my cake got sprinkles all over her boss?"

He patted my cheek. "No. Have you been thinking that this whole time?"

"I..." That was exactly what I was thinking. "She left so soon after the cake, I thought she must have..." I shook my head.

"She wasn't," he assured me. "In fact, you did her a favor. Her boss was so angry about all the sprinkles, she was more honest with Mom than she would have been. And you know our mother. She had a hard time working with someone like that once she knew the score."

"I'd be angry too if I had sprinkles spilled over me," I said. "Just like you were angry when you were covered in glitter."

"Which wasn't me, by the way," Blake interjected quickly.

Cam glanced over his shoulder to his teammate. "Yeah, well. I better get back to my wife." He quickly gave me their order and disappeared back into the delivery room.

Blake stood and wrapped his arms around me. "So, all this time you thought you got your mother fired. That's why you don't like practical jokes."

"I told you it was stupid." I leaned my cheek against his shoulder.

"It's not stupid," he said. "If I did something that turned out badly, I'd feel bad too. Maybe even bad enough to never pull another prank again. I understand why you don't like them." After a moment he asked, "What colour were the sprinkles?"

I laughed softly. "Rainbow. I wasn't going to waste chocolate sprinkles on something like that."

"Can you teach me how to make a hollow cake?" He leaned back and smiled.

"So you can recreate it?" I asked. "It didn't go so well the first time, remember?"

I wasn't there to see it, but from what my mother said, it made a bigger mess than the dickfetti Blake placed over my office door. It sounded like carpet was involved. I wouldn't have wanted to be the one to clean it out. Although, I probably should have, since it was my cake to begin with.

"Then we do it right this time," he said.

"I'm not pranking some innocent person again," I said.

"Who said anything about a prank?" Blake said. "I told you, I keep my promises. This would be something completely different."

I gave him the side eye. "We can talk about it. But first, let's go and get something for the parents-to-be to eat." I could hardly believe my brother would be a father in a matter of hours. How was he old enough for responsibility like that?

Okay, who was I kidding? I'd never see him as old enough, or responsible enough to be a parent. He was my brother, I wasn't supposed to see him that way. Honestly though, he was going to make an amazing dad. And Andi was going to be an incredible mother. With any luck, the kids would look like her, not him. With her brains. Would Cam even wait until the kid was old enough to walk before they were on the ice, hitting a puck? Probably not. He'd probably bought a stick and a few plush pucks already. Or a hockey themed mobile to hang over the crib.

One thing I knew for sure, the kid would never lack for love. After all, they had the best aunt in the world, right? In fact the two best aunts in the world, because Andi's sister, Pia, was pretty epic in her own right.

"Deal." He leaned in to brush his lips over mine. "No ice cream and pickles."

"Definitely none of that." I kissed him back, his mouth warm and sweet. "I'll leave that to whoever pranked my brother." Now I was picturing him digging into ice cream with tiny chunks of pickle buried inside. If that actually happened, I hoped to be around to take a photo of the expression on his face. It would be priceless. Thinking about it made me want to laugh out loud.

"We need to find out who that is," Blake said. "And whoever sent you those notes."

The reminder of my secret admirer brought me back down to earth. I'd been able to forget about that for the last few hours. Now, it came crashing like a mud slide, threatening to engulf me.

Having told Blake about the cake was cathartic, but the relief was overshadowed. It couldn't completely nullify the relief in knowing I hadn't caused my mother to get the sack. I made an assumption and it was wrong. For ten years, I lived with it, nurturing it and letting it grow until it almost had a life of its own.

Now, I could stomp it down until it was nothing.

Because that was what it was—nothing. Okay, not to Mom's former boss, but in the scheme of things it was.

I tried not to think too much about the fact I could have simply asked my mother. If I did, I'd feel pretty silly for never bringing it up. Not to mention she might feel bad for not explaining.

Ugh, Cam was never going to let me forget this, was he? Lucky I had that photo. That might keep him from bringing it up too often. I *knew* that bribe would come in handy. I made a note to store a copy in a safe place, in case he decided to try to delete it. Knowing him, that's exactly what he'd do. Dispose of the evidence before anyone saw it. I'd have to be sure to choose somewhere he'd never think to find it. If he was anything, it was persistent. He'd go on looking until he found it. Let him look. Things like this were exactly my jam.

"He might have given up," I said finally. The glance we exchanged told me he didn't believe that either.

I exhaled softly.

"Come on, let's go and get some food." Blake laced his fingers through mine and we headed out of the hospital and into the late afternoon sunshine. "Later, I want to have something to eat." He gave me a look that sent heat straight to my core. "We might find a nice, empty hospital room."

"If you're not careful, I'll sidetrack you before we go and get food," I warned.

"I wouldn't mind a bit," he said. "But we should get food first. To build up our strength."

"Yes we should," I said. "But only because my brother would notice if we take too long."

"And we would take a long time," Blake said. "I intend to take all night."

Chapter Twenty-Six

Blake

We barely got inside before I picked her up, wrapped her legs around my waist and pressed her against the door. I slanted my mouth over hers and kissed her long and slow. Like I said I would, I wanted to take my time.

"We should..." she said against my mouth.

"Be careful? I'm all over it." I cupped her ass to hold her in place before sliding my tongue between her lips.

She kissed me back but then pulled away and glanced around. "I was going to say make sure Vivian isn't standing in the kitchen."

"Oh, good point," I said.

Holding Alice carefully, I turned around for an exaggerated good look.

"The coast is clear." Her roomie's door was closed and the apartment was silent.

"Maybe we should take this to your room," I said at the same time as she said, "We should go to my room."

I laughed and kissed her forehead before carrying her into her room and pushing the door shut with my foot. Cam said Andi was going to be in labor for hours yet, so we wouldn't be interrupted at least until morning. That should give me enough time to show her how I felt. I needed her to feel like a princess.

Like she was my favorite hockey stick, I carefully laid her down on her bed and flopped down beside her, bouncing a couple of times.

"This is comfortable," I said before rolling onto my stomach and placing a hand beside her head, so I was lying over her. Our lips met again, deeper this time. She tasted like the Thai food we both ate for dinner, spicy and delicious.

"Blake," she whispered between kisses. "Are you sure?"

I pushed myself up on my elbow and regarded her. She looked back at me, eyes dark and intense, her brow creased slightly. Unsure but absolutely fucking gorgeous.

Absolutely fucking *mine*.

"I've never been more sure of anything in my life," I said. "But if you don't want to..."

"I do want to." She pushed herself up to kiss me. "I wanted to for a long time. I just..."

"Wasn't ready?" I brushed hair off the side of her face and kissed the tip of her nose. "Thought I might have used my last packet of condoms as glitter-filled water balloons?"

"I'm not going to say the thought hadn't crossed my mind," she said slowly, a smile creeping onto her lips.

I grinned. "My second last packet maybe, but not my last packet. My last packet is all for us."

"What color was it?" she asked. "The glitter, I mean."

"You really want to talk about water balloons right now?" I touched the side of her chest with the tips of my fingers, inching them down her skin and under her sweater. I kissed her again while I worked them under the cup of her bra and over her nipple. Her sensitive nub tightened at the touch.

"Not really," she admitted.

She grabbed the hem of her sweater and pulled it up over her head before throwing it aside. After a moment, her shirt went the other way, leaving her in a pale pink, lacy bra, sheer enough to make out her rosy nipple under the fabric.

"Do you know how beautiful you are?" I whispered. I stripped out of my own sweater and shirt before unbuttoning her jeans and sliding them down her hips. Exposing the long expanse of her legs bit by bit.

"Maybe a six on a good day," she said.

I stopped with my face just above her pussy and frowned. "Alice North, you are not a six. You're a thirteen and five-sixths."

"That's very specific." She picked up one foot, then the other to help me slide her jeans off.

"I have a favorite number and a favorite fraction," I said with a shrug. "You happen to fit both of them." I pushed off my track pants and lay beside her in my boxer briefs. Yes, they had cartoon characters on them. What else would anyone expect?

"I've never been anyone's favorite fraction before," she said.

"Get used to it," I said. "You're my favorite fraction and my favorite cardinal point." I eased down the cup of her bra and started to work on some other special points.

She sat up to unhook her bra and slide it down her arms, giving me a view of perfection.

"You're stunning," I whispered. I gripped her panties and pulled them down before she kicked them aside. "Absolutely perfect."

"Have you seen yourself?" She rolled onto her side and ran a hand down my abs, one by one as if she was counting them. She stopped with her hand splayed across my stomach before slowly, tentatively ghosting over my erection. "You're gorgeous."

I quivered under her touch. If she wasn't careful, I was going to come in my boxer briefs. Right around the spot where a cartoon cow was printed.

"Alice," I whispered, just to say her name.

"Blake," she whispered back. "This might be my favorite point of *my* favorite cardinal point." She peeled down the top of my boxers until my cock was fully exposed. Pre-cum already leaking from the tip.

"You like my East-wood?" I asked, smiling, even though my balls ached for her.

I used to get teased at school before I pointed out I had big feet, therefore I must be in proportion. I suggested they refer to me as Bigwood, but it didn't catch on. Shame, I could have used the ego boost back then.

Alice snorted softly before stroking her fingers up and down my length. "I like it very much, but it's more central than it is East."

"Yeah, but it points to the East," I said, nodding down to my cock.

"Huh, you're right," she said, continuing to stroke me gently.

"If you keep doing that—" I rolled her back onto her back and worked my way down her body, kissing and licking until I reached the apex of her thighs. I parted them gently and lowered my face between them.

"You smell amazing," I said. She tasted even better. I stroked her carefully and slowly with my tongue, working her with my fingers until her back arched and she cried out my name.

"God, Alice, you always come beautifully," I said reverently. I could watch her come all night, even if I didn't get off myself. I didn't care about that as much as I cared about her feeling good. Again and again and again.

"You are beautiful," I added, kissing the inside of her thighs before working my way back up her body.

"You make me feel beautiful," she whispered.

"I want to make you feel like you're a thirteen and five-sixths," I said, teasing her navel with my tongue. "I want you so much."

"I want you too," she said. "Please."

I kissed her mouth, letting her taste herself

before leaning over the side of the bed and pulling a condom out of the pocket of my track pants. I tore it open with my teeth and tossed aside the foil.

"Can I do that?" she asked. She took the condom from my hand and sat up to roll it down my length.

"You have magic hands," I told her. "But I don't want to come in them."

She gave me a cheeky smile before adjusting the condom, making sure it was in place and then smoothing down the sides as if it needed that.

"We want it on just right," she said, her eyes sparkling.

"Alice North, you're a tease." I took both of her hands and pinned them above her head before straddling her hips. "You know what I do to teases?"

"What do you do?" She brought her legs around my hips, pressing her entrance against the tip of my cock.

I lowered my face until I could whisper in her ear. "If they're beautiful, I fuck them nice and slow." I pushed the head of my cock inside her, just slightly. Letting her warmth gradually engulf me like we became one person.

"And you are the most beautiful woman I ever saw, so for you it'll be extra slow." I pushed in a little deeper. "Fuck, you feel incredible. The perfect fit." Nice and tight.

"You're so big," she said softly, visibly relaxing as I stopped to let her adjust to my size. "At least thirteen and five-sixths."

"You're so tight," I whispered. "Like two pieces of a puzzle made to fit together."

"I'm not a puzzle," she said.

I knew she meant she wasn't complicated, but she was wrong.

"You absolutely are," I said. "A puzzle. An enigma. One I want to spend a long time trying to decipher."

I suspected the rest of my life might not be long enough and I was okay with that. We didn't have to know every tiny detail about each other, just the important ones like what it took to make her come.

"Blake," she moaned.

There were no more words between us, just slow, careful strokes of my cock inside her and of my thumb over her clit until she came again. Only then did I let myself go, losing myself inside her, perfect bliss that lasted and lasted. Better than I ever experienced before in my life. Bliss I wanted to feel over and over. Bliss I wanted to give to her every night.

I flopped down beside her and gathered her into my arms.

"That was even better than I dared to hope for."

"It was for me too," she said, suddenly sounding shy.

"No regrets?" I smoothed sweaty hair from her brow with the pad of my thumb and kissed her temple.

"None," she said. "Except..."

My heart stuttered for a moment. "Except?"

"Except we should have done it sooner," she finished, fully aware she'd managed to get a rise out of me.

"No, we shouldn't," I said, letting my heart slow. "Like you said, you weren't ready. Tonight you were." If we'd done this sooner, she might have wished she hadn't. I didn't want that for her. For either of us.

"Just when I think I've figured you out, I really haven't," she said. "You're also a puzzle."

"I'm one of those one thousand piece puzzles that have been scattered on the ground and a few pieces misplaced," I said with a laugh. "They probably got eaten by someone's puppy. Or pecked apart by a duck."

She laughed softly. "Only you would say something like that."

"I don't know, I'm sure a few people would say that *about* me," I said. "I'm happy to own it."

"You are, aren't you?" She rolled over to face me.

"Unashamedly," I said. "Theory has it, us goalies are a different breed. Some suggest we've all been dropped on our heads. Who else would volunteer to stand in front of a fast moving, hard piece of rubber? Me? I call it living my best life."

"Do you think I could be so carefree?" she asked.

"Do you want to be?" I asked. "I happen to think you're pretty incredible the way you are." I didn't want her to change, but if she wanted to live life more freely, then I'd be happy to help her.

"I could take more risks," she said thoughtfully.

"What do you have in mind?" I raised an eyebrow at her.

Before she could answer, her phone loudly announced an incoming text message, the tone cheerful, like a piano.

"That's Cam's text tone." Her expression changed to one of worry before she leaned over the edge of the bed. Hanging so her ass was in the air as she searched for her phone.

Pulling it out of the back pocket of her jeans, tapped on the screen.

"Oh."

She looked from it to me.

Chapter Twenty-Seven

Alice

"He's so tiny," I said softly as I stared down at my newborn nephew. He was the image of Cam, but with a mop of dark red hair.

"Ten little fingers, ten little toes," Andi said with a tired smile.

"He's perfect," I told her, barely able to look away from him for long enough to smile at her. I bent over to kiss the tip of his little nose. "Obviously he got that from his mother."

"I'm not going to argue with you there." Cam sat on the side of her bed. He looked almost as tired but proud as hell. "Both him and his mother are the best."

"You're pretty special yourself," Andi told him.

I wrinkled my nose. "You're not going to get mushy are you?"

Truthfully, they were adorable together. No one could deny they were head over heels for each other. And now they had this little one, who was going to have all of us wrapped around his little finger. Okay, he did already.

"Yes, we are." Cam leaned down to kiss Andi. "We've been talking about a name."

"Have you decided on anything yet?" I asked.

"Of course, they're going to call him Blake," Blake said from where he hovered beside the door. "Middle name, Blake."

Andi laughed. "We love you, but we're not naming the baby Blake Blake North."

"That sounds like some weird version of Duck, Duck, Goose," I said, laughing.

Blake grinned. "I think it sounds awesome, but I guess Andi is lacking taste in the baby name department."

"I don't like it either," Cam said dryly. "Andi went through every baby name website in existence, but thanks for the suggestion."

"We wanted to get it right," Andi said. She shifted, trying to get comfortable, but nothing seemed to help. "Cam wanted to name him after his favorite sports stars. As much as I like the name Alex, we have enough As in the family. Same with Marc-Andre."

Cam shrugged. "Andi wanted to name him after her favorite book boyfriends."

"I like that approach," I said approvingly.

"Please tell me his name is Dracula," Blake said eagerly. "Or better yet, Frankenstein. Frankie for short."

"Blake Blake is sounding better and better," Cam said.

"Don't humor him," Andi told him. "No, I wanted Kai or Evan. Or Cooper. Or Levi. Or Asher." She sighed. "I have a lot of favorite book boyfriends."

I glanced up at her and smiled. "Me too."

Although, if I wasn't careful Blake would become a real life boyfriend. So far, he was better than a book boyfriend. My satisfied clit happily reminded me of that.

"Are you going to keep us in suspense?" Blake asked. "What name did you choose?"

"Same question." Pia Welling swept past him into the room, flowers in one hand a teddy bear in the other. "There's my little nephew." She handed the flowers to her sister, the teddy to my brother and turned to smile at the baby.

"Would you like to hold him?" I asked, offering him to her.

She waved her hand at me. "Plenty of time for that. You enjoy him."

"My sister isn't a baby person," Andi said.

"I don't want my own babies," Pia said easily. "I like other people's babies just fine. Especially ones as cute as him." Her expression softened when she looked down at his sleeping face.

"So, what is his name?" I asked. "Dracula North does have a ring to it." I gave Blake a sly glance.

"This is what I'm saying." Blake grinned.

"If you want to be known as Dracula, we're happy to accommodate you," Cam said to me. He raised a finger and pointed it at Blake. "Don't say anything about sucking."

Blake raised his hands to either side in surrender. "I wasn't going to say a word." He gave me a wink.

I shook my head at them both. "Andi, what did you call him?" Maybe I'd get a sensible answer out of the Sea Dragons' owner.

"We decided to name him Matthew," Andi said. "Matthew Cameron North."

"Hey, Matt," I whispered to the sleeping newborn. "Welcome to the world. You're a lucky kid. You're already surrounded by people who care about you. Just some words of advice. Take after your aunts, not your daddy."

I glanced up at my brother to see him rolling his eyes but grinning at the same time.

"I think that advice is perfect," Pia said. "Between you and me, we'll make sure he turns out okay. Andi too, of course."

"And me," Blake said. "I can teach him how to tie shoelaces."

"You're not going to teach him how to tie other people's shoes together," Cam said.

"If you'd prefer to teach him that, I'll find something else to teach him," Blake said, unruffled.

"Don't make me get a restraining order," Cam said without any heat.

"If you don't mind, I'd like to take some pictures for the team's social media," I said. "Not of his face," I added quickly.

When it came to the organization as a whole, this was big news. It wasn't every day a defenceman became a father, much less with the team's owner. Like it or not, people were going to want to know the baby was born and was healthy.

"I was thinking I could take a couple of photos of his feet and hands," I added. "Nothing else. And none of either of you, because this is private time. I'll tell them he's arrived and is doing well. And that we'll keep them updated when you're ready."

But not before.

Cam didn't look happy, but eventually he nodded. "Fine. Just feet and hands, that's all. We don't want him becoming a circus."

"I'll make sure he doesn't," I said. Big news or not, I wanted my nephew to have a normal life, as out of the spotlight as I liked mine. More so, because the risk of people wanting to know about him was higher than any interest in me. His parents' profiles were much higher than mine.

"Here." I handed the baby to Pia before taking up my phone and teasing the blanket away from one of his tiny feet.

"That might be the cutest thing I've ever seen," Blake said, peering over my shoulder. "Apart from his aunt, of course."

"Thank you," Pia said, pretending she thought he was talking about her.

"You too," Blake said, giving her a smile. "Of course, the new mommy is adorable as well."

"I don't feel very adorable right now," Andi said, shifting again.

"I'll do this quickly so we can leave you to get

some rest," I said. She'd need as much sleep as she could get for the next few months. Okay, years.

"Lucky the next game is at home," Blake said.

"And the one after that," Cam agreed.

They'd have to win the third game before there'd be a fourth, but I appreciated his confidence. I took a quick photo of Matthew's foot before tucking it back into the blanket and taking a couple of photos of his curled up fist beside his ear.

I glanced at the photos to make sure they looked good, and nodded. "Perfect, just like him. I'll post these up as soon as I get to work."

"Thank you, Alice," Andi said. "I'm glad we brought you on board with the team. You've been a great asset to the Sea Dragons."

"It runs in the family," Cam said, eyeing his son.

"He's only just been born," Andi reminded him.

"It never hurts to encourage them from the start," Cam said.

"Encouraging is fine, pushing him is not," she said. "He might decide to be something else instead of a hockey player."

"Like something out of your books?" Cam teased. "Let me guess, mafia don? Stalker? Baseball player?"

"He might be all of the above," she replied, unfazed.

Cam snorted. "My son is not going to be a base-ball player." His expression was deadpan while he waited for us to absorb what he said and laugh.

"You hear that?" I said to the baby. "Your daddy is okay with you being a mafia don."

I wasn't going to mention stalkers. The reminder was an unwelcome one again.

"As long as he can support his parents, he can be whatever he wants," Cam said. "Including baseball player. He might grow up to be a pitcher for the Sea Cucumbers."

"I just want him to grow to be happy," Andi said. "And preferably law abiding."

She gave me a quick glance to indicate she remembered the secret admirer too. It was just like her to worry about someone else only hours after she'd given birth. She was one of the most caring people I'd ever met. My brother was lucky to have found her.

Grudgingly, I admit she was lucky to have found him too. As brothers went, I could have done a lot worse.

"Admit it," Blake said. "You all want him to grow up to be a goalie."

We all turned to look at him. He grinned and shrugged. "What can I say? It's a calling."

"Right now it's probably calling you to be at training," Cam said.

Blake looked down at his phone. "As a matter of fact, yes. I should get going."

"Me too," I said. He'd driven us here. I'd need him to drop me back at home so I could get my car.

"So you two are together?" Pia glanced up from the baby to look from Blake to me and back again.

"Yeah," Blake said before I could respond. "Yeah we are."

"Nice." Pia drew the word out, nodding her approval before turning her attention back to the baby. She made faces at him while he opened his eyes and stared sleepily in her direction.

"We think so." Blake draped an arm over my shoulders and kissed my cheek.

"You two are adorable together," Andi said.

Cam grimaced. "Now who's getting mushy?"

"Nothing wrong with a bit of mush," Blake said unapologetically. "You might have noticed we arrived together. First thing in the morning."

He didn't need to paint a picture of what we did last night, his not so subtle suggestion was explanation enough. He wasn't going to flinch at it and neither was I. We had nothing to be ashamed of and I had no regrets. If he did, he was hiding them well, but I was certain he also had none. People like him never did. How had he described it? He was living his best life.

"I noticed, but I was pretending not to," Cam said.

Andi gave him a meaningful look. "We're happy for you, aren't we, Cam?"

Before he could say anything, she turned back to us. "You have our full support. Not that you need it, but you have it anyway. I can't really object to my employees getting together with each other, can I now?" She gave my brother a soft look.

"You could," Blake said slowly. "I'm glad you're not going to. Otherwise I'd have to ask for a transfer, or early retirement."

"It's that serious?" Cam narrowed his eyes at both of us, his brow wrinkling.

"Not yet," I said quickly. "We're taking it one day at a time."

"And one night at a time," Blake agreed. "We still have to figure out who sent Alice those notes and cupcakes. We have a building to save and we have playoffs."

"Exactly," I said. "We're in no hurry."

"None at all," Blake said. "We really should go; the boss might yell at us if we're late."

"Your coach might, your boss won't," Andi said tiredly. "I've done enough yelling for a while." She looked like she could hardly keep her eyes open.

As cute as baby Matthew was, bringing him into this world was clearly exhausting. She had my sympathy as well as a slight hint of envy. He really was the most adorable baby. Of course, I'm not biased in any way toward my nephew. He happens to be that cute.

"We'll let you get some rest," I said, backing toward the door. "Let us know when you go home and we'll drop in and check up on you there."

When had 'I' become 'we'? I didn't know, but it felt normal, natural.

But like he said, we had a lot on our plate before we could relax and move ahead together.

Chapter Twenty-Eight

Blake

Like so many professional athletes, I had my routine and my superstitions. So when I grabbed my helmet, ready to warm up before the playoff game and found it full of Jell-O, I was thrown off.

"What the hell?" I stared down into the red, transparent, wobbling mess, oozing out.

"What is it?" Flynn glanced over my shoulder. "Uh..."

"What?" Nate moved over beside him and took a look for himself. He snorted a laugh.

"It's not funny," I said softly. At any other time it might be. Okay, it would be. But before a playoff game on our home ice? Not a chance.

Flynn put a hand on my shoulder. "No, it's not. Can you wash it out?"

Of course I could, but that wasn't the point.

"This wasn't meant as a joke," I said. "Someone is trying to piss me off."

"Looks like it's working," Nate observed. "That's a dick move on game day."

"No shit," I said, angrier than I intended.

"Save it for the ice." Flynn patted my shoulder before stepping away. "Get it cleaned out and forget about it for now."

It was good advice from our captain, but easier said than done. I turned around, searching the faces around me for any sign of guilt or amusement. Everyone was busy taping their sticks and adjusting their padding. Mostly moving around in silence, lost in their own thoughts or mantras.

"Is this supposed to be some kind of payback?" I asked Flynn, keeping my voice low. "Because I never would have done something like this during the play-offs. Or any other game, especially an important one."

"I know you wouldn't," he said. "They over-stepped. Try not to let it get to you. We don't want you off your game."

"You don't," I said. "But someone does." I might have blamed the opposition, suggested one of them snuck in here. I didn't want to think anyone would stoop that low.

If it wasn't them, then who was it?

"Don't let them win," he advised. "Roll with it like you always do."

He was right, I always did. I cracked jokes, not jaws. Even as a kid, when the others were teasing Robbie and I wanted to punch them in the face, I didn't. I'd distract them by doing something ridiculous. Anything to draw the attention from him.

I won't say I haven't swung my share of punches on the ice, because I have, but not off the ice.

I gave a sharp nod and stepped into the restroom to wash my helmet under the sink. Frustrated at the waste of Jell-O as it disappeared down the drain. Slightly less frustrated at the fact my helmet would smell sweet and fruity until I started to sweat. I might start a new trend. Air freshener for hockey helmets. Starting with raspberry fresh.

I rinsed out the last of the Jell-O and stepped back into the locker room to grab a towel and wipe out the inside of my helmet. As I did, I caught sight of one of the equipment guys. He glanced at me before hurrying away.

I frowned at his back. He seemed familiar, but I couldn't place him.

That, I decided, was a problem for future me. Present me finished drying and tossed the towel in a basket before trying to get my brain back into game mode.

"The old Jell-O in the helmet trick, hmmm?" Nate grinned. "For the record, it wasn't me."

"It wasn't me either," Cam said. He stood beside Nate, wearily rubbing his forehead with the heel of his hand. "I haven't had enough sleep to think about doing shit like that."

"No one thought you did," Nate told him. He glanced toward Zack, but the right winger had his head down, taping his stick and ignoring us. Nate shook his head.

No, I didn't think this was Zack's style either. He wasn't a fan of me, but he wouldn't sabotage us by messing with my equipment. He'd risk sabotaging himself if he did. We didn't work as hard as we did, only to fuck it up on purpose.

"Let's concentrate on kicking ass," I said. I couldn't help running through a list of who had access to the locker room while I pulled on my padding and laced up my skates.

The image of the rapidly retreating equipment guy kept popping into my head. If he was involved, there was nothing I could do about it now.

Almost nothing. I was careful to check every bit of my equipment. None of it seemed to have been tampered with. I triple checked my mask. If there was a problem with that, it could end painfully. Whoever messed with my helmet was trying to mess with my head, not get me injured.

I hoped.

I'd pissed off my share of people in my life, but not enough for any of them to want me hurt. I made a point of having the equipment manager check my blades to make sure they were secure and sharp.

"Feeling the pressure, Eastwood?" he asked with a knowing smile. Like a lot of the guys who worked for the team, he was a former player.

"You know it," I said. "I'm feeling the weight of the whole city on me today."

That wasn't far from the truth. Most of Lowball Bay would be watching. Many counting exactly how many goals I let through. If we lost, I'd be the first person they'd blame. I'd also be the first person *I'd* blame.

"The whole city is behind you and the rest of the team," he assured me. "We're ready for a big celly." He checked my skates and nodded his approval before stepping back.

"We'll do our best not to let you down then," I said.

I loved the pressure. Thrived under it. The more, the better. Knowing Alice was out there, ready to cheer me on? That made it even sweeter.

For half a second, I wondered if she was the one who put the Jell-O in my helmet, but I dismissed it immediately. She'd spent too many years blaming herself for her mother switching jobs. If we lost tonight, she'd blame herself for that too. That was a risk she wouldn't take.

"You won't," the equipment manager said. "It's the Sea Dragons' year to go all the way. And if you don't, there's always next year." He gave me another nod before hurrying off to attend to something else.

"He's right, you know," Nate said. "This is our year. I can feel it. And our girls are watching. It's like the whole universe is aligning." He raised a hand above his head and moved it slowly in an arc, mimicking the movements of the stars. He lowered his hands and grinned, giving a sideways look to Flynn.

Flynn gave him an expressionless glance before pretending he needed to adjust his padding.

I cocked my head at Nate. "You really think him and Valentina..."

Nate raised his gloved hand. "As sure as I'm

standing here. Something is going on between those two."

I reached out, swiping the air in front of him, pretending I was going right through him. "Who said that?"

He gave me a playful shove. "I'm not a ghost, dickhead. I am, on the other hand, a betting man. How much do you want to bet on them getting together?"

"What time frame?" I asked.

Nate looked thoughtful. "Twelve months. Maybe less, but you know Flynn. He likes to take his time."

"I know you're talking about me," Flynn said without looking up. "You're barking up the wrong tree. There's nothing happening between me and Valentina." He pulled on his gloves without meeting either of our eyes.

"A hundred bucks." I held my hand out to Nate.

Grinning, Nate shook it. "I look forward to taking your money. I'm surprised you'd bet against them getting together in a year."

"I'm not," I said. "I'm betting it'll take them six months." I'd never seen Flynn so evasive about a woman before. Not that he flaunted his hookups, but there was definitely something between him and the coach.

"You both suck," Flynn said without any heat.

"But you still love us," I said.

"Maybe I do," he said. "Maybe I don't. Let's get out there and warm up."

"Aye, aye, Captain." I gave him a salute with my catcher and followed the other guys out onto the ice and into the roar of the home crowd.

The first face I saw as I stepped out of the tunnel was Alice, her phone on us, filming us as we passed, one by one.

She gave me a smile. The kind of smile that was just for me. A smile that told me how much she cared about me.

I leaned to the side and waved to the camera, clowning around like usual. What can I say? It was how I liked to let off steam. If I made a few people laugh along the way, then it was more than worth it. And if a few people thought I was a dork, that was okay too. Life was too short to worry about it either way.

She shook her head, but didn't stop smiling as she filmed my antics.

"Do you have any words for the fans?" she asked.

She hadn't asked anyone else that question as they went past. Of course, most of them were still in their own heads. And of course, she wasn't their girlfriend. But there was more to her question than that.

She saw the way I cared for the people around me. The way my speech the other day inspired people. Before her, I'd only seen myself as a goalie who loved life. But now? Now I realized I could be an inspiration to the people around me. I had the potential to be influential.

If I wanted, I could be influential as puck.

"I just want to tell everyone to keep smiling and live their best, authentic lives." I gave a 'rock on' gesture to the camera before blowing a kiss and starting to move past to let the others onto the ice. Before I was out of earshot, I said to her, "This game is for you, baby."

I caught the flush of her cheeks before I had to look away and step out onto the rink.

I waved to the crowd before starting to warm up, skating off to the side and kneeling on the ice to do the ever-popular groin stretches.

I smiled to myself, knowing Alice was watching. Was she imagining herself as the ice under me? If she wasn't, I was. I pictured her stretched out, her naked skin slick with sweat. Imagine the way she sounded when she came with me deep inside her.

Focus, I told myself, grateful for my cup that hid

my growing erection. That was the kind of embar-
rassment I didn't need. Not in front of a capacity
crowd and all the TV cameras.

I got back to my feet and skated in front of the
goal, ready to stop the puck my teammates slapped
in my direction while they too warmed up. A couple
came in a little harder and faster than necessary, but
I heard Valentina call out for them to dial it back.
They didn't want to risk injury while warming up.

Wait a moment.

I frowned to myself. The answer came to me in a
snap. I knew where I remembered that equipment
guy from. He was Kyle Parkinson, the player Alice
used to date. The one who was injured out by over-
doing it.

It was him. He was the one who sent her those
notes and cupcakes. He was the one who put Jell-O
in my helmet.

The game started as I figured it out, and there
wasn't a damn thing I could do about it.

Chapter Twenty-Nine

Alice

THE FIRST PERIOD ENDED WITH THE SEA Dragons down two to one. The goals Blake missed weren't easy ones by any means, but he seemed distracted from the moment the game started. I had no idea what was going on, but he wasn't at his best. Was it because I spoke to him before the game? I could have put him off without realizing. If we lost this because of me...

While the teams took a break, I took the opportunity to go to the toilet. Social media would have to do without a few minutes of the guys drinking water and shooting the shit between periods.

I dried my hands and stepped out of the restroom, almost running into someone in the corridor.

"I'm sorry." I looked up. "Kyle, what are you doing here?"

"I work here," he said, as if somehow I should have known that.

I didn't know everyone who worked for the organization, but I would have noticed if I'd seen him around.

"As of when?" I asked. The intense way he looked at me, brown eyes unblinking, was making me uneasy. I stepped back, out of his space.

He stepped forward, back into mine. "As of a couple of weeks ago. I've been keeping a low profile. I wanted to give you some space. Looks like I gave you too much."

"What are you talking about?" I asked. A couple of weeks? How had I not seen him around? I'd been distracted, but not that much.

He leaned his hand against the wall beside my head. "I'm talking about you and Blake Eastwood. You've been getting cozy with him."

I shook my head. "Yeah, I have, so what?"

"So, didn't you get my notes?" he asked. "My presents? Is this how you treat people now? You throw gifts back in their face?"

I stared at him, frowned so hard it almost hurt.

"You were the one who sent those things. And paid for my lunch."

"You're welcome," he said sarcastically. "In return, I get to see you walking with him." He yanked his phone out of his back pocket, tapped on the screen and held it out.

I saw myself, walking back to the arena with Blake, my face pale. Our hands were clasped together, bodies close.

"Yeah, and?" I asked. What did he want from me? He and I ended a long time ago. He used me to get close to my brother. Now he wanted...what? To get back together?

"I screwed up," Kyle said slowly. "I didn't tell you how much I cared about you. I let you walk away. I got the job here so I could be closer to you. I sent you those notes so you'd know how I felt. I would have given you as much time as you needed."

"I had no idea it was you who sent them," I said. "I thought it was Blake until he said—"

"*Blake*," Kyle spat. "As if he'd do something like that. The guy is an idiot."

I bristled with irritation. "Blake is one of the sweetest, nicest people I've ever met. He'd never use me to get close to someone I was related to. Or for any other reason."

"Are you sure about that?" Kyle sneered. "Isn't he using you to save that stupid building? Isn't he using you to make himself look good so he can get endorsements? So he can retire comfortably?"

"No," I said simply. "He's not like that."

"Open your eyes, Alice." Kyle snapped his fingers in front of my face. "You deserve better than someone like him. I bet it never crossed his mind to send you anonymous letters. Does he know what your favorite cupcakes are? Would he find out where you're eating lunch and pay for it? Has he done any of those things?"

I pushed his hand away. "No."

Blake knew better than to send me anonymous notes, having seen how much they freaked me out.

"And he never will," Kyle said with certainty. "Because he'll never feel what I feel about you. I never stopped caring about you, Alice. I should have come right out and told you, but I thought you'd like the romantic gestures. I know you. You like to be romanced. I knew you'd get a kick out of the secret admirer thing. Does he know that? It seems to me like he doesn't have a clue."

"Of course he does," I argued.

"What has he done that's romantic?" Kyle asked. "Name one thing."

"There's more to relationships than romantic gestures," I hissed. "Not being an asshole, for one thing. If you'll excuse me, I have to get back to the game."

I turned away from him. He reached out, curled his fingers around my shoulder.

"Get your hand off her," Blake growled.

He stood in the corridor behind me, his mask pushed up off his face. His skates made him that much taller. He stalked towards us, eyes on both me and Kyle.

Kyle dropped his hand to his side and took a step back. "You don't appreciate her like I do."

"Firstly, that's bullshit," Blake said. "Secondly, were you the one who put glitter in Cam's shampoo?"

"Annoyed you didn't think of it?" Kyle sneered.

Blake snorted. "*Please.* I can prank a better prank than that any day. Why did you do it?"

"Because I wanted you to take the blame," Kyle said. "I heard the gossip. You promised Alice you wouldn't do anything until after the playoffs were over."

"You wanted to make trouble between us?" I asked.

Kyle shrugged one shoulder. "Sooner or later, he's going to hurt you. I figured this would make it sooner." He didn't even seem slightly repentant. Just like when we broke up. He wasn't sorry about using me to get to my brother either. He didn't care who he used to get what he wanted.

"The Jell-O in my helmet?" Blake accused.

The what? I stared at him, then at Kyle. Kyle straightened his shoulders, looking smug as fuck.

"To screw with your head," Kyle said. "It worked, didn't it? You played like shit all game." He tipped his head back, looking at Blake down his long nose. As if somehow he was the one scoring points off Blake.

I remembered that arrogance from when we were dating. How had I ever found him attractive? He was self-centered and insecure. Always trying to get one up on the people around him to make himself feel bigger. If he hadn't injured out of the NHL, he'd be a hundred times worse now, his ego stroked by fans and puck bunnies, not to mention his own success. Evidently the universe only took him down a couple of pegs. He still seemed to have plenty to spare.

I wanted to wipe the smile off his face and kick him in the groin. If I wasn't worried it might get me fired, I would have. Andi would understand, right? Of course, it might force her hand, and he wasn't worth it.

"It's not over yet," Blake said evenly.

He didn't seem rattled by the accusation. If anything, he seemed relieved to be having this conversation. He must have figured out Kyle was behind everything and when I didn't come back to the rink, he came to find me. Was this the distraction of me that put him off his game?

The old Alice would have blamed herself. The new, more confident Alice blamed Kyle. If he hadn't started all of this, it wouldn't be a problem to begin with. He'd tried to get into Blake's and my heads, but we were done with that. Both of us. Everything was out in the open now, the air cleared.

"The game isn't over," Blake said for clarification. "This conversation is." He stepped over closer, getting up in Kyle's face. "You're going to stay away from my girlfriend. You don't speak to her unless she wants you to. You don't look at her. You don't think about her." He jabbed a gloved finger into Kyle's chest.

Girlfriend? We hadn't talked about that, but I liked the way it sounded coming from his lips.

Girlfriend and boyfriend. Some day, maybe more. I was his and he was mine.

"You don't send her anything else," Blake continued. "You know what'll happen if you do? You think red Jell-O in a helmet is a badass move? Let me tell you, it's amateur hour at grade school. If you put a foot out of line, I'll make sure you spend the rest of your life looking over your shoulder for cream pies to hit you in the face. Not the fun kind. You'll never dare to put your shoes on again without checking for shaving cream." He jabbed his finger in again.

"You'll never get into bed again without wondering if this is the time you'll find a fish's head under the blankets. Yes, I said a fish's head. I don't believe in killing horses. Also, fish get really, really smelly. If you're lucky, I'll throw in an onion or two. Maybe some horse shit to round it out." He looked as though he was very seriously contemplating buying some right now and finding Kyle's address.

"You're out of your mind," Kyle told him. His eyes were wide. Bordering on scared. He was buying every single word out of Blake's mouth.

Blake grinned. "I absolutely am. Out of my mind and head over heels for this woman. I also don't make idle threats. I can and will make your life a living episode of *Candid Camera*. Understood?"

Kyle raised his hands to either side and backed up. "Fine. If this is the guy you want?" He glanced at me quickly.

"It is," I said. "It really is."

"You're both out of your minds," Kyle said. He shook his head, turned and hurried away.

"Chickenshit," Blake muttered.

"Shaving cream in shoes?" I asked, biting back a smile. If any one of us was out of anything, it was going to be Kyle, out of a job. I'd have a word to the GM or Andi as soon as I had the chance. Unless Blake beat me to it.

Although, if Kyle had a lick of sense, he'd quit first. What was he thinking, working here to get close to me? He really seemed to think I'd take him back.

He was delusional.

And trying to make me think Blake wasn't romantic enough? He was, in his own way. I didn't need fireworks or flash mobs.

I needed him.

Honestly, it probably wasn't about me anyway. I didn't care what his real agenda was, as long as he stayed away from me. I had no doubt he would now. He got the message I wasn't interested.

I had no idea why he'd believe I was, but that was over and done with now.

Blake chuckled and wrapped his arms around me. "It's a classic, but a good one. I might do it anyway." His gaze followed Kyle until he disappeared around a corner.

"Can we forget about him?" I asked. "We need to get you back to the ice for the rest of the game."

The break would almost be over by now. They'd be wondering where both of us were. Okay, Blake in particular. They had a backup goalie, of course, but they'd want him there, playing or not. Boosting morale as only he knew how. Maybe he should become a mascot when he retired from playing. I suspected he'd love that.

"I'd rather stay here and fuck you, but someone is going to come looking for us," he said reluctantly. He leaned down, picked me up, threw me over his shoulder and started off at a run. "Once more, into the breach!"

Chapter Thirty

Blake

"Well, that sucked." Nate flopped down beside us in a booth at Shells, pulling Oaklyn down beside him.

"You can't win them all," I said, pulling Alice onto my lap to make room. After playing like crap the first part of the game, I was on fire for the rest. Nothing else got past me, but we also didn't manage to score on the opposition. We put up one hell of a fight, but in the end we couldn't pull the Win.

"I want to win them all," Nate said. "But at least I have you." He smiled softly at Oaklyn, who returned the look in equal measure.

"Awww, you two are almost as cute as me and Alice," I said. It was obvious to anyone they adored each other. I'd given Nate shit for saying he changed his ways, but he proved me wrong and I was here for it. Seeing them happy was worth it.

"In your dreams, Eastwood," Nate said. "No one is cuter than me and Oaklyn. No offense, Alice."

Alice shrugged and took a sip of her bourbon and cola. "None taken. You two raised the bar pretty high."

Nate leaned forward, his elbows on the table. "Would you say we're cuter than Cam and Andi?"

"Let's just say we're all adorable and leave it at that," Oaklyn suggested. "I'm going to go and get another drink. Coming, Nate?"

"I hope so," Nate said. He grinned and gave us a wink while Oaklyn shook her head at him. Holding hands, they headed for the bar, where Brody Clutterbuck was dispensing drinks and sympathy.

"I'm sorry," Alice said, nestling against me.

"What for?" I asked.

"If I figured out sooner that Kyle was behind all of that, he wouldn't have done what he did to you," she said. "Distracting you like that, it's..." She shook her head.

"Completely his fault, and mine," I said. "He shouldn't have done what he did, but I let him get to me. But you know what? I'm not going to blame myself for us losing tonight. The Sea Dragons are a team. Every single one of us played the best game we could. The other team played better. It happens. Next time, we'll whip their asses and serve it to them on a platter. I might even throw some fish heads on there for them."

I squeezed her gently. "You're not responsible for his actions or mine. Okay?" I stroked the back of my hand down the side of her cheek.

"I know," she said. "I just wish I'd seen it sooner."

"Me too," I said. "But it's over now and he'll leave you alone."

"You'd really do those things to him if he doesn't, wouldn't you?" she asked.

"I won't have to," I assured her. "You don't have to worry about me putting shaving cream in his shoes."

"Just other people's shoes," she said.

"Never yours," I assured her. "And I'd never pull anything like he did. Messing with a guy's equipment is not cool. Especially on game day. My favorite kind of Jell-O too." I pouted playfully.

"We'll make you some more Jell-O," she said. "I'll put that on the list for our celebration party."

"For coming second?" I asked, slightly confused but appreciative. If she wanted to throw us a runner-up party, I was here for that too. Any excuse for having a good time.

"No, for after the council meeting," she said. "When we win against the developers and the building doesn't get torn down."

"Right," I said slowly. I'd forgotten about that with everything else going on. Now she reminded me, I couldn't help a seed of nerves from planting itself in my brain and starting to grow. Losing the playoffs sucked, but losing that building would be devastating for future generations.

Yeah, there were more important things in life than hockey. Who knew?

"Can we have a piñata?" I asked.

She laughed at the hopeful expression on my face. "If you want. We can get a nice big one for you boys to beat the crap out of." She mimed beating a floating piñata with a big stick, her lower lip drawn between her teeth in concentration. Fuck, she was cute.

"I can give you a nice big one," I said in her ear. I ran my hand over her stomach, down to her thighs and between her legs.

"I know you can," she said, shivering slightly.

"Alice," I said slowly. "There's something I've been meaning to tell you."

She had been looking at my hand, but she raised

her gaze to my face. Her expression completely dead-pan, she said, "You really prefer green glitter?"

I tipped my head back and burst out laughing. "Actually, I prefer dickfetti. Especially when it's all through your hair." I cupped to the back of her head and kissed her forehead. "That wasn't what I was going to say though."

I took a deep breath and lightly kissed her mouth. "I love you, Alice North."

She blinked at me a couple of times but smiled and kissed me back. "I love you too, Blake Eastwood," she said.

"You do?" I asked. "Thank fuck for that, other-wise this whole conversation would have gotten really awkward." Not that I expected her to say it back, but I was glad she had. Those words coming from her lips, they made my heart light and my dick hard.

She batted me on the chest with the back of her hand. "You're one of the silliest people I've ever met, but you're also one of the most caring and sweet. You enjoy life. I want to enjoy my life with you."

"I want that too," I said. "You're the most beauti-ful, smartest, passionate woman I've ever met. And you saw right through my clown mask, and saw who

I really am. And you didn't run away, which is a bonus."

"Are you going to start pranking again?" she said with a sigh.

I shrugged. "Probably, but I'll tell you about them first so you can film them. I might give up my plan for world domination though. I'd rather spend the rest of my life with you."

She laughed. "Thank goodness for that. I'm not sure if the ducks would ever recover from being involved in something like that."

"Exactly." I nodded. "We really needed to think of the ducks. And the geese."

"I thought you liked geese," she asked.

"I do, when they're not chasing me," I said. "But I prefer you." I kissed the tip of her nose.

"It's nice to know where I stand compared to geese," she said jokingly.

"You're much better than a goose," I assured her. "Much better than anyone else I know." I pressed my forehead to hers, enjoying the way it felt to hold her like this.

"Blake," she whispered.

"Yeah?" I whispered back.

"Can we go home now?" she asked.

"Your home or mine?" I asked. Since Kyle was

dealt with, I could go back to my apartment if I wanted to. Honestly, the idea made my heart sink. Even if I slept on her couch, being close to her was enough. Okay, almost enough. At least I was in her space.

We told each other how we felt, but that didn't automatically mean she wanted to go on living like that.

She picked her head up and looked at me. "I want to grab each day by the balls and live it."

"I want to help you do that," I said slowly. I wasn't quite sure where she was going with this, but I was along for the ride. Literally and figuratively.

"Is it too soon to look for that house we talked about?" she asked. "The one near the ocean with a swimming pool?"

I went to grab my phone out of my pocket. "We can start looking right now if you like."

She put a hand on my wrist. "Tomorrow is fine. Or the day after, because it's already tomorrow."

She was right. It was already Sunday morning and the council meeting was on Monday. Somehow we'd squeeze in house hunting around that.

I pushed my phone back into my pocket and wrapped my arms around her. "If you change your mind in the morning and want to wait, that's okay too."

She smiled softly. "How are you real?"

I pushed my sleeve up far enough to pinch myself.

"Just checking I actually am real. In case this is all a dream. For the record, that felt real. You can try if you like." I offered her my arm.

She grabbed my wrist and brought my hand to her lips before kissing my palm. "You feel real to me. I guess I got lucky."

"No, I'm the lucky one," I said. "Come on, let's get out of here before the other guys decide to sidetrack us." On another night, I wouldn't mind, but tonight I wanted to be alone with her.

I helped her up off my lap and wrapped my arm around her as we made our way through the crowds and out into the early spring morning. Only a couple of cars passed while we walked to her place. The city was otherwise quiet. Quiet enough to hear the waves hitting the beach half a mile away. Every now and again, laughter would burst out of Shells, but other than that, it was us and the stars.

"This is nice," she said softly.

"Yeah, it is." I kissed the top of her head. "Next

season, we win. Then after that, I might think about retiring."

"Yeah?" She looked over at me. "Then what will you do?"

"I don't know," I admitted. "Maybe I'll learn to ride a unicycle. Maybe I'll take you on holiday to meet the geese in Stanley Park. See if they're nicer than the ones in Toronto. Walk around the harbor in Vancouver. Or throw a few coins in the slots in Vegas. Or walk on a beach in the Bahamas. Or have that pizza in Chicago with sausage stuffed inside. We could do all of those things."

"I've been thinking of opening my own PR company," she blurted out. "I've been thinking about it for a long time, but I was too scared to chase that dream. Now... If I don't chase it, what am I doing with my life? It's not going to come to me."

"If that's what you want to do, I'll support you all the way," I said. "Maybe I could tag along and carry your laptop."

"You wouldn't be bored doing that?" she asked.

"If I'm with you? Hell no," I said. "I'd love every minute of it. But I want to squeeze in a few dreams of my own. I'd like to teach kids with disabilities how to skate and play hockey. Disadvantaged kids too. Equipment can be expensive and if they can't afford a pair of skates, they can't chase their dreams. I might start a foundation or something."

"The Blake Eastwood Foundation," she whispered. "I like the sound of that."

"I think you found your first client," I said. "You're hired to run the social media for the foundation."

"I'd be honored," she said with a sniff. "You'll need an office."

"I know a place," I said. "The space above the Ballet Academy is currently empty. Once the council votes to save the building, I can rent it and set up there."

"Then they better save it," she said. "Because that sounds perfect. Close enough to the arena for coaching, as long as you're allowed to use it for that. I might be able to help there. I know the Sea Dragons' owner and her husband. I might be able to pull some strings."

We both laughed. It sounded like the perfect dream.

If only the council vote went our way.

Chapter Thirty-One

Alice

"It looks like all of Lowball Bay is here." I had to speak up to be heard over the hum of voices in the room.

"Yeah, it does." Blake swiveled around in his chair to wave at someone behind us. "It looks like Joe brought all of the Sea Cucumbers here too."

I turned and followed his gaze to see Joe Santoro standing by the door. Beside the pitcher was his teammate, Fisher Ellison. Beside him, I recognized his brother, Gabriel Ellison, a local businessman. He stood with his arm around a dark-haired woman, saying something in her ear.

"And the Humpbacks," I added, as Hawk Florence stepped past Joe, his wife Becca in tow. A few of Hawk's teammates trailed behind them. They were followed by a few of the Starfish, the city's PWHL team.

"I've thrown parties with fewer famous faces showing up," Blake remarked.

"They didn't know what they were missing." I leaned into him.

"That's what I've been telling them all these years," he agreed. "Maybe they'll get it now." He spread his hands to indicate the entire gathering.

"Who knew saving a building was all it took to bring all these people together?" I said.

"To be honest, I had a suspicion," he said. "I'm going to have to find another building to save after this. For the good of my social life." His body shook as he chuckled.

"I don't think your social life is hurting," I said. "But I don't object to trying to save all the old buildings in Lowball Bay. The ones that can be saved, that is." Some of the older ones were dangerous and needed to be torn down. But the ones that could stay standing, should.

"This will set a precedent," Blake said softly. "If we lose today..."

I straightened up and cupped his cheek with my hand, feeling his stubble under my palm.

"We won't lose. How can we, with so many

people behind us on this? Look at all the people who turned up to support you and Linda. Everyone here today is here because of you. Because you spoke out about something that was right."

"If I hadn't, someone else would have," he said.

I raised a single eyebrow at him. "Since when are you humble? Maybe someone else would have said something, and maybe they wouldn't. And you did. That's what matters. You brought all of these people together for something important. If you ask me, that's pretty heroic."

"I should have brought my cape," he said, the corners of his mouth turning up.

"You don't need one," I said. "Besides, that would have given the goose something to grab on to."

He laughed. "You're right. Remind me to buy one for Nate." His eyes shone with humor. Of course he wouldn't want his friend attacked by a goose either.

"You're not going to start wearing your underwear on the outside of your pants, are you?" I asked jokingly.

He cocked his head at me. "Only in private."

I laughed. There really was no one else like Blake. As long as I lived, he'd keep me laughing at silly things, clowning around when I was sad and needed a pick-me-up. When I needed someone to turn to, he'd always have my back, and I'd have his. We didn't need world domination, we just needed just to save the special places a little bit at a time.

"That's an interesting fantasy," I said in his ear.

He whispered back, "My fantasies involve a lot less clothes. And no underwear. Although, I wouldn't rule out a cape."

I giggled. "For someone who wanted my nephew to be named Dracula, that doesn't surprise me."

"Does that mean we can't name any of our kids Dracula?" he asked, his expression deadpan.

I hadn't thought about kids, but this was something that should be addressed and put aside immediately.

"No Dracula," I said firmly. "No Frankenstein. No Cthulhu. Definitely no Medusa. Or Thor, for that matter."

He nodded slowly with each name. "Okay, noted. Kraken it is."

I batted his chest with the back of my hand. "Not that either."

He grinned and kissed my mouth, only pulling away when the room started to fall quiet.

"Thank you everyone," the Councilwoman called out, silencing everyone further. "We have to start with the formalities, but we'll get those out of the way and focus on what you're all really here for." She took her seat, and a man rose to call out the minutes and apologies for absences.

"I'm glad I don't have to attend meetings for a living," Blake whispered in my ear. "I'd end up putting laxatives in everyone's coffee to end it sooner."

I bit my lip to suppress a laugh. "Of course you would," I whispered back. "Do you do that during team meetings?"

"I haven't," he said slowly. "But now you put the idea in my head..."

"You're incorrigible," I told him.

He grinned. "It's all part of my charm." He draped an arm over my shoulders and pulled me closer.

"Yes, it is." I nestled against him.

The longer the meeting went on, the more my nerves started to fray. I knew they had to do all the formal stuff, but I wished they'd get on with it. Blake started to jiggle his knee, suggesting he was as anxious. Under other circumstances, I would have asked him to stop, but I understood how he was feeling. He had to let it out somehow.

"All right, now that's out of the way." The Councilwoman rose again. "Let's get to the matter of the

Ballet Academy building on Eel Street." She clasped her hands in front of her. "As you can imagine, we had a lot to discuss. What's best for Lowball Bay economically, socially, historically and even educationally. The proposal for more housing was a viable one. No one can deny we all need a place to live." She smiled around the room as people shuffled, some muttering with preemptive annoyance.

"However." The single word plunged the room into a thick silence.

"We unanimously agreed that the historical value of that particular building could not be ignored. Therefore, we have decided to approve the application to have the building registered as a historical structure that will remain part of Lowball Bay for at least the next few hundred years."

Blake leaped to his feet, pulling me with him before throwing his arms around me and shouting victoriously.

"We did it! We did it!"

Tears overflowed down my cheeks as I hugged him back. "Yes, we did. You did."

He leaned back and placed his knuckle under my chin to lift it. "I couldn't have done it without you. We did this." He pressed his lips to mine and kissed me as the crowd went wild with relief and excitement.

Blake was right. Who needed world domination when you could save it, a bit at a time? This was just the start.

I didn't know where it would end, but I knew we'd be doing it together.

Epilogue

Blake

"A ND THIS SEASON, WE'RE WINNING THE Eastern conference and the Stanley Cup," Cam concluded as we waved at cameras before stepping through the doors into the arena.

"Yeah we are," I said. "We're going to nail this season right from the start." After spending the off-season hunting for the perfect house with Alice and moving in with her, I was feeling fit and ready. Like everything else fell into place, and now it was time for this.

"Damn right we are," Nate agreed. "We came so close last time it hurt."

"Speaking of hurt..." Cam was looking at something behind my left shoulder.

For a moment, I thought he was trying to prank

me. Tricking me into turning around before someone threw a water balloon at me. Or hit me in the face with a cream pie. Or—

The possibilities were endless.

Then I realized the expression on his face was not only serious, he looked concerned. Deciding it was more or less safe, I turned around.

Flynn Weston was making his way towards us. One foot was in a moon boot and he was leaning on crutches.

"What the hell did you do?" I asked.

"I don't want to talk about it." He kept on going past us.

"Wait, you can't *not* talk about it." I hurried to catch up. "How long are you going to be out for?"

He stopped and looked over at me. "I don't know yet. Maybe you should ask Valentina." Without another word, he headed into the meeting room, leaving us to gape behind him.

"Well shit," Nate said softly. "This isn't the start to the season I expected."

"Yeah, me either," I said. What the fuck had happened and what did Valentina have to do with it?

Bonus Epilogue

Alice

"Wнат?" I caught Blake staring at me as he carried the covered tray.

"A couple of years ago, you would have said this is a bad idea," he said with a grin.

"Do you want me to say that now?" I asked. "We could always take that home." I turned and took a step back the way we came.

"You don't want to do that any more than I do." He laughed. "Come on, this is going to be great."

Shaking my head, I followed him up the front pathway and into the open door of Cam and Andi's huge house.

We found a place about ten minutes away from them, so we could walk back and forth from family dinners and get-togethers. I got to watch my nephew get bigger and take his first steps. I was there when he became a big brother to my second nephew, also not named Dracula.

"Aunt Liss!" Matthew couldn't quite manage Alice yet and I had a suspicion his nickname for me might stick, but it was adorable. Almost as cute as his nickname for Blake. "Uncle Bake!" He toddled towards us on his chubby legs, his arms raised to be picked up.

"That's right, Uncle Bake baked a cake," Blake said.

"Cake!" Matthew's face lit up.

I had to hold him carefully so he didn't reach for it. "This is a special cake," I said. "Don't worry, you'll get some cake." Just not this one.

We made our way out to the backyard, where it looked like half of Lowball Bay gathered, waiting for us.

"Here's the happy couple," Cam said, coming over to give me and his eldest son a hug.

"Thank you for agreeing to host our gender reveal," Blake said. "We figured this was the perfect place for everyone to get together. Any excuse for a pool party." He eyed the balcony above the pool.

"Don't think about it," I told him.

He grinned and placed the tray on a table placed

beside the pool for this moment. "Would I jump off the balcony into the pool?"

"Yes, you would," I told him. I suspected that was why he wanted to have this here and not at our house. We had the swimming pool he always wanted, but not to the convenient balcony for jumping off.

He waited until I put Matthew down before putting his arms around me and giving me a kiss. "I have something for you."

"You're in public," Cam pointed out.

Blake chuckled. "Not that. Something else." He pulled something out of his back pocket and handed it to me. A piece of paper folded in half.

"Open it," he said.

I glanced at him before unfolding the paper and starting to read.

I don't tell you enough how much I love and appreciate you. You mean more to me than anything in this world. More than winning the Stanley Cup. More than saving all the buildings. More than having a house with a swimming pool.

. . .

I glanced up at him and shook my head while smiling.

"Priorities," he said with a laugh.

I looked back down at the note.

As long as I keep breathing, I'm going to keep on loving you and doing my best to make each day special. Your not-secret admirer.

"That's so sweet," Andi said. She'd come to stand behind us, holding Liam, my younger nephew, in her arms.

"I'm only crying because I'm pregnant," I said, wiping tears from my cheeks.

"Get used to it," Andi said. "Pregnancy hormones are wild." She leaned over to kiss my cheek.

"Should we find out if we're having a boy or girl?" Blake said.

He uncovered the tray to reveal a tall, purple frosted cake. "I vote Uncle Cam should do the honors." He picked up the cake slicer and offered it to my brother.

Cam eyed it suspiciously. "Nope. Not a chance. I know you better than that, Eastwood."

"Would your sister pull a prank on you?" Blake challenged.

Now Cam eyed me with suspicion. "I suppose not."

"Of course I wouldn't," I said. "I'd be honored if you'd do this for us."

Cam gave me the side eye for a few moments before taking the slicer and stepping over to the table. "Don't make me regret this."

Blake and I exchanged smiles before I caught Andi's eye and grinned. She made a face and stepped over closer to us.

"Cake!" Matthew shouted.

Before any of us could stop him, he barreled into the table, hands out in front of him. He made a grab for the side of the cake, his fist closing around just enough for it to collapse. A tsunami of pink sprinkles poured down out of the cake, all over him.

For several moments, he stood there with his mouth open, arms still above his head, looking surprised. Then he started to laugh and laugh.

"Sprinkles!" he declared. He stuffed his hand into his mouth and started to suck them. They were all through his hair, his clothes and the ground around him.

"You suck," Cam said to Blake and me, but he

was smiling as much as the rest of us. "Congratulations."

Blake wrapped an arm around me and pulled me to him. "Thanks. We're excited."

"I'm sure you are," Cam said. "You're going to need the practice. You can start by cleaning up my son."

"That balcony is looking good," Blake said. "Can you film me, Alice?"

I hesitated, torn between cleaning up a mess and enabling him. Finally, I nodded and pulled out my phone.

"Go on then. Just be careful."

He grinned. "I always am."

I knew he would be. He had too much to live for. We both did.

Thank you so much for reading! If you loved Blake and Alice's story, please leave a review.

What's next for the Sea Dragons? It's time for Flynn and Valentina's story in For the Love of Puck.

About the Author

Freya M. Love writes steamy romantic comedies with guys we like to swoon over and women we can relate to. All wrapped up with a snort-worthy bow that comes with no guarantee you won't spit out your drink.

Buy paperbacks direct from me My Store
Join the fun of Freya's Lovlies on Facebook! Join!
Subscribe to my Newsletter.
Follow me on Pinterest.
Follow me on TikTok.
Follow me on Amazon.
Follow me on Bookbub.

Also by Freya M. Love

Lowball Bay Sea Dragons

Not the Puck Bunny

Personal as Puck

Influential as Puck

For the Love of Puck

Lowball Bay Humpbacks

Game Plan

Playing Field

Offside

Goal Line